ALPHA KNOWS BEST

A SOUTHERN SHIFTERS NOVEL

ELIZA GAYLE

GYPSY INK BOOKS

ALPHA KNOWS BEST

A Southern Shifters Novel

eliza@elizagayle.com
http://ElizaGayle.com

Malcolm Gunn stopped breathing at the shift of air in his house. His eyes popped open when the fur prickled along his forearms, warning him of the intruder nearby. He'd gone to bed hours ago but something had kept him from falling into a deep sleep and now he knew what.

Someone had been hunting him and was now in his home.

Nose to the air, he took a slow deep breath, seeking the scent of a hunter.

Cougar. Familiar.

The scent was unmistakable, one any other of his kind would recognize right off the bat. His eyes slid closed as he allowed the smell deeper inside while he sought an answer to what he faced. Definitely not one of his brothers but still a cougar. He couldn't help but wonder what idiot would be so brave as to enter the lair of a black cougar without permission. He'd easily be within his rights to kill on sight with no questions asked. Yeah, if he was still part of the clan. As an outcast no one gave a shit about him and any aggression toward another cougar could easily lead to a visit from one of his brothers, The Death Enforcers.

He brushed his fingers across the hair on his chest to relieve the prickling another's presence in his house created. The scent had a distinct underlay to it besides the basic aggression that always lay just underneath the surface of a were cougar on a hunt. A sudden flash of sweet reached him then and his body arrowed up from the bed, his bare feet landing silently against the hardwood floors.

A woman prowled his house. And not just any woman.

Malcolm crouched low to the ground, careful not to disturb the airflow around the room. Better not to let her know he was awake and lying in wait for her. He'd give her a little more time to get closer. His hand slid back underneath the single pillow on his bed and wrapped around the hilt of the hunting knife that he kept there. Nowadays the weapon was mostly used for gutting animals he'd caught, but habit made him keep it for protection as well. He had no idea what her intentions were but he wasn't about to face her unprepared. It had been a long time since he'd had to kill a person and while the animal in him remembered it occasionally, the man didn't miss it at all.

He listened for any telltale sign that would indicate her location. Nothing, as he'd expected. This woman knew what the hell she was doing. A floorboard ten feet from his bedroom door creaked quietly. He smiled slowly, a surge of satisfaction spreading through him. But she wasn't better than him. The air in the house stilled again as he imagined her waiting and listening for any indication that he'd woken from the soft sound she'd made. He'd designed and created that little trap himself and if she'd been human she would never have heard it.

Would she keep going? By now, she would have followed his scent to this room, but no way in hell would anyone ever get through that door without waking him. If this was the woman he suspected, and his body screamed it was, she'd know that and be prepared. He glanced behind at the window over his bed and decided to approach this in a different way. If she wanted to play cat and mouse he'd be more than happy to oblige her—except, like it or not, she was about to become the mouse. He crept to the window and raised it without a sound, just enough to give him room to slip out.

Malcolm inhaled the night air deep into his lungs. The scent of earth and moisture clung to everything around him. This was his favorite time of the night, those quiet hours shortly before the rest of the world woke up. Nature was at its peak power during this period. She could overpower and overcome anyone she wanted at any given time but when Mother Nature rested along with the rest of the world, his animal longed to roam.

He slipped into the cover of trees that surrounded his temporary home. A feature he'd used to his advantage more than once these past weeks. The wet grass slipped cool under his feet and the cat ached for freedom.

Not yet. He couldn't risk the pain.

He struggled to soothe the restless animal inside him. *First we confirm the identity of the woman stupid enough to enter our home, then when she's taken care of we'll take care of our needs.*

Emerging from the forest, he crouched outside the side door that led through the garage and listened. As best he could tell, she still hadn't breached his bedroom but he needed to hurry because there was no telling what her plan was. The bitterness of a brewing betrayal clawed at his gut. He'd honestly hoped he'd never have to see her again. At least on a conscious level.

He slipped through the dark and around his Land Rover with ease. Not only did he know this layout like the back of his hand, he didn't need light to see. A cougar's vision meant he saw in crystal clear clarity with or without light so not much got past him just because it was dark outside.

He turned the knob and opened the door into the house. He'd not moved an inch and her sweet smell washed over him. While his brain worried about an unwarranted attack, his dick stood up and took notice, making it damned hard to think straight when all the blood in his body pooled into his groin and his pulse beat for the not-quite-a-stranger roaming his house.

Get a grip. He seriously doubted she'd come for the long overdue fucking.

But it had been a long time since he'd been with a female of his own species. For a while, he'd toyed with some witches that liked to dance on the dark side but even he'd grown bored with that after a while. While he enjoyed his fair share of trouble, there were just some things nature didn't intend for you to mess with and sooner or later she would fuck back.

He looked down to see he'd tented his shorts and he cursed the loose boxers he'd chosen to sleep in. This was all he needed. He'd grab her and she'd either laugh at her effect on him or find a way to use his condition against him. There were a dozen scenarios of how this could play out running through his head as he padded through the kitchen on his way to the living room. From the middle of the room he would be able to see the full length of the hall that stretched out in front of the three bedrooms in his house.

Malcolm slowed his steps, knowing he wouldn't get much closer without being detected unless he controlled his breathing as well as his movements. He waited for his heartbeat to slow and his breath to slide in and out of his nose on a soft, barely there whisper.

The knife hand dropped to his side, still at the ready but not overly threatening as he took the two steps to where they would be forced to come face to face. Except—fuck. She wasn't there. No way did she slip through one of the bedroom doors without him detecting her.

"Looking for me?"

He whirled at the sultry voice behind him in time for her to deliver a kick to his stomach, catching him off balance and sending him flying backward to sprawl on the floor. Air whooshed from his lungs and his head cracked against the hard floors. Pain exploded in his head, little shards of sharp, burning sensations that took hold for several long seconds before clearing.

Stunned that she'd snuck up on him, he groped for his bearings. The little minx took full advantage of his delay and pounced on top of him, straddling his legs with her own. He didn't even see the knife until she had it pressed to his throat and dangerously close to his jugular.

"What's wrong? Cat got your tongue?"

Malcolm slowly dragged the air back into his lungs and wondered what kind of crazy bitch she'd turned into. The power emanating from her came soaked in strength without even a whiff of fear. For a second or two, he felt frozen in time. This woman looked nothing like the Chey he remembered. This woman had obviously trained and his instincts screamed she would not be an easy fight. Interesting.

Her white blonde hair was tied up in a braid but a few strands had come loose and curled around her face. His fingers itched to brush them from her cheeks. With the anger in her eyes and the stern shape of her mouth, she reminded him more of the women from his clan than ever. In an act of aggression, she bore resemblance to the cougar more than ever.

"My tongue's just fine, Chey. Want to find out?"

The look in her blazing eyes flared hot, shining in the moonlight as she speared him with her gaze. Electrifying pools of blue that a man could easily get lost in. All but a few shifters had green eyes and he'd only heard of one kind that had blue. He curled his lip at the memory.

The elusive white cougars.

Half-breeds that no clan wanted except for their dirty work. While he and his brothers carried out death sentences in accordance with the laws and traditions of their councils, her kind had trained for a different kind of mission. They'd become mercenaries available to the highest bidder. They used methods of stealth that he and his brothers rarely bothered with. They didn't need to.

"In your dreams, Malcolm."

Over the years he'd allowed his perception of her to soften. Maybe she was different. Obviously not, considering the position he now found himself in. There was nothing soft about the blade cutting into his skin, or the strength in which she pinned him with her free hand. Obviously the only emotion she'd developed outside her family was anger. It probably made her missions easier.

He growled warningly. "Then get the hell off me."

"Or what?" Her hand tightened its vise tight grip on his arm and pinned him to the ground, a position he wanted her in right now. If he thought her scent had been enticing, that was nothing compared to the body heat infusing him as she sat atop him thinking she had him under control. From the moment she'd set foot in his house, she'd set their course in motion. It was only a matter of time.

With her hair pinned back, he stared at the pale expanse of her bare skin like a moth to flame. His teeth ached with the need to sink into the sweet curve of her neck and taste.

Goddess, get a grip.

Clearly it had been too long. Mate or not, there was no excuse for the extreme reaction his body had toward her. If she slid back an inch or two she would know too. His raging hard on had not eased in the slightest since he'd first scented her. Not even the subtle smell of the wolf on her deterred him. Oh no, instead he hurt like fucking hell, throbbed actually from wanting her. He needed to get his little half-breed off him and now.

Before he did something crazy like start shredding her clothes.

"I don't want to hurt you... but I will." Although he imagined his idea of hurting her and her ideas would likely differ drastically. The kind of pain he had in mind could bring the most mind numbing pleasure if given half the chance.

"I wouldn't lay odds on that if I were you. I'm not the same woman I was all those years ago."

"So I gather. Doesn't change the danger. Or the warning." The last time he'd seen her, he'd been so angry that fate had fucked them hard. He'd had a duty to his family to uphold the laws and traditions of their kind, and mating with a woman who had wolf blood in her veins would have landed them both at the receiving end of a death sentence.

"Yes, Malcolm. I haven't forgotten a single, disgusting, hate-laden word that came out of your mouth that night. Why do you think I have a knife at your throat?"

His body tightened further at the sound of his name coming from her mouth. And what a mouth it was. Full and pink standing out against the porcelain color of her skin, *lush* was the word that came to mind. So pale it practically glowed. The anger running underneath meant little to the man or animal anymore.

"So you do know what you've started here then?"

She shrugged and scrambled off him. "I'm not here to start anything so don't go getting crazy ideas in your head. I simply needed to make sure I had your attention before you did anything stupid. I'm not here because I missed you. There is an actual purpose to this little surprise reunion."

Already missing the heat of her body pressed to his, he pushed himself to a sitting position, willing his dick to behave. "And what exactly is that?"

He stood to his full height of six foot three and loved the fact he didn't tower over her. When he finally got inside her again their bodies would fit together perfectly. He bit back a dark smile. So much for that hard on going away. Although it was the prickling at his skin and simmering desperation in his veins he really worried about. He gritted his teeth against the oncoming pain and allowed it to wash over him. The pain of his body being denied its natural process had almost become second nature. A low growl rumbled through his chest. She had no idea the danger she toyed with by coming here, but she was about to find out.

"Kane sent me."

While not surprised at all, it wasn't the revelation he'd been hoping for. Anger seethed through him at the memory of his last encounter with his brother. They'd fought and it had ended badly and over a woman no less. A woman in his mind who didn't deserve his brother's time. When exactly had his family fallen apart? Every single one of them had found their mates only to discover nothing but heartache and trouble. Lucas and Kane had given in to mating heat. He had not.

He wasn't sure he could walk away a second time but he had to try before he hurt her. The feral animal inside had affected the man.

"Not interested." He turned toward the hall and headed back to his room. The mention of his brother had helped his situation a little, but he figured if she didn't leave soon, no mention of Kane, Lara or Chey's half-breed status would hold back his restraint to the lovely creature standing in his living room. Much more and he would need her as much as he needed air.

"Wait. What do you mean not interested? I haven't even finished what I had to say."

Malcolm moved in a flash, grabbing her by the shoulders and shoving her to the wall. "Don't say I didn't warn you."

The animal inside him clawed and cried to get out. Her scent was driving him crazy. With one hand, he grabbed both of her wrists and raised them above her head. He used the weight of his body to pin her in place before grabbing the rope tethered to the wall.

"Dammit, Malcolm. This isn't what I came for and you know it."

"Oh yeah?" he snarled. "Then how come I can smell the sweet scent of your arousal?" His voice came out harsh and growly—more animal than human. With the dexterity of a man who knew his way around rope, he tied first one wrist and then the other before he released his hold.

"You're being unreasonable."

Malcolm slammed his pelvis against hers, making sure she got the full effect of how hot her presence made him. "Am I? Really?" With her hands tied above her head, her breasts thrust invitingly toward his face. His claws protracted and he snagged the edge of her shirt with the tip. Slowly, he began to slice the offending garment away. "Tell me to stop," he dared. The sharp tip of a claw lightly scraped across a clothed nipple.

Instead, she whimpered, the luscious sound of her submission music to his ears. He skimmed one hand down her side and pushed his fingers between their bodies. Her hot flesh seared his fingertips before he slid them under her waistband. When he skimmed the downy hair covering her mound, he imagined her all those years ago laid out before him, offering herself to him. For a brief few seconds, he circled her clit before dropping to her slick opening. Before she could utter a sound, he pushed two fingers deep inside her.

She gasped.

"You're so damn hot and wet right now, sweetheart. I think you'd let me do anything I want to you," he purred into her ear. His head buzzed with need so strong his vision hazed. All the while his fingers toyed with her until he hit the bundle of nerves guaranteed to send her over the edge. His teeth nipped at her neck as he worked her over nice and slow, taking care to prolong the building pleasure as long as possible. He massaged her clit and felt her chest heave as her release raced dangerously close. When her breathing hitched and perspiration broke out on her body, he removed his hand.

"No coming unless I give you permission, Chey. You know the rules." For his own sanity, he took two steps away from her. The pain in his head warred with the pain in his body. The cat abhorred being caged and reminded Malcolm of that fact every chance it got. In the face of its mate it was even worse.

"I'm going to get dressed." He disappeared into the other room and then into the closet. His arms and legs trembled with the force of denial he didn't have the strength for. He needed to fuck her so bad he thought he'd die from it. But the man in him refused. Not until she begged.

He grabbed a pair of faded jeans and quickly slid them up his legs over the briefs he'd worn to sleep in. He searched through the drawer for a clean T-shirt when she stuck her head inside. Again, everything about her surged through him. He took shallow breaths in and out of his mouth, avoiding her scent. If he got even a hint more of arousal they'd both be done. It became imperative that he get her out of his house and as far away from him as possible. He'd leave here tonight.

"You're still mean as ever, Malcolm, you know that."

Shocked, he turned and caught her gaze. "How the—"

She held up her hand and showed him the tiny knife. "You didn't really think I'd come in here unprepared did you?"

Crafty. He liked it. "You can go back and tell my brother whatever it is, I'm not interested. I'm not a part of the clan anymore and I'm not interested in their bullshit." A sudden, dark thought struck panic in his heart and he turned to face her.

"Nothing has happened to Kane or Lucas right?" He eyed her warily, concern clouding his judgment.

She shook her head. "They're both healthy, but serious trouble is on the horizon. Lucas is still gone and Kane may be on his way out now too."

He held up his hand to stop her. "No, don't tell me. I really don't care. Their politics is none of my business."

"Your brother asked me to find you and bring you home, and you think that's none of your business?" He heard the shock and annoyance coming from her clear as day but he didn't—no, he *couldn't* care. Too much time and trouble had passed between them all, and in his condition he had no choice but to let go of the past. It was the only way he'd keep what little of his sanity he still possessed.

He shoved the drawer closed and stomped his way from the closet. For every step he took in her direction, she took one step back. The lack of fear in her gaze challenged him, made the animal stand up and take notice. She hesitated in front of his bed and images of her spread out and tied to the four posts invaded his thoughts. She had the perfect body for a little bondage play. He could imagine that pale skin of hers pinking up quite nicely after a thorough flogging from him. Would she scream for mercy from his darkest desires or embrace them with her own?

Damn.

On a groan, he shoved the images of her beautiful skin from his mind and turned to walk out the door. He'd noticed the oh-so-subtle change in her breathing as he'd watched her move toward the bed. Her eyes had dilated. He no longer needed his sense of smell to acknowledge her arousal.

"You need to get out now before it's too late," he warned on a harsh growl. His teeth elongated and dug into the corners of his mouth. The animal fought for freedom, and if Malcolm could release him he would. Consequences be damned. As it was, with the cougar partially trapped, Malcolm had a few precious seconds of control left to save them both.

"Malcolm, please."

If he took what he wanted it would be against her will. Mating heat was one thing, really wanting him another. He was a bastard but he wasn't ready to go that far...yet. She'd made her desires to not be mated to him crystal clear. Her sudden appearance did nothing to wash away the years of hate he'd harbored right alongside the need. That it was mostly hate for himself mattered little at the moment.

"If you don't get out of my house right this minute, you'll find yourself backed against the wall with my dick buried inside that sweet smelling pussy before you can even think to pull that knife again. Is that what you want?"

Her eyes grew wide an instant before she backed out of the room and hustled to the other side of the house. Unable to resist, he stalked after her.

At the front door of his home, she twisted the locks loose and wrenched it open. Malcolm held his breath for the relief her disappearance would give him when she suddenly turned back.

"Your family should be more important than your anger with me. Kane needs you. There are lives at stake."

A sound resembling a laugh and a snarl emitted from his throat. "You can tell Kane you found me and that I refused his request. He'll still pay you, sweetheart."

"It isn't always about the money."

"Sure it is, darling. Don't be naïve. Now get the fuck out. Whatever Kane's problems are, they're no longer my concern. That ended the moment they escorted me off clan property."

Fury darkened her features when he motioned her out, a look that did nothing to dampen the arousal beating at his insides. From his experience, anger often led to some of the hottest and most violent sex two people could share. And he could well imagine her giving him a run for his money in a fight. She had to leave *now* before he lost what little control he still managed to maintain.

"I won't leave. I have my orders, and one way or another you will go back with me."

In a lightning fast move, Malcolm grabbed Chey and wrapped his arms around her waist, pulling her against his body. The sudden move gave her no chance to protest. His mouth slanted across hers and his tongue plunged between her parted lips as she tensed against him. He'd planned a hard, demanding kiss to frighten her, but with the first taste of her hot little mouth, he didn't want a quick sample. Malcolm slid his tongue against hers, savoring her unique flavor that unfolded into his mouth one layer at a time. When her body softened in his arms, relaxing against his chest, he deepened the kiss.

Chey opened to him a little more and he sank deeper than before. He teased her tongue with licks and scrapes of his teeth, his fingers pushing through the braid holding her hair to the back of her head. God help him, he couldn't get enough. He craved. Ached. Needed it all.

His gut clenched at the dizzying sensations flooding through him. Her small hands traversed the planes of his chest and shoulders, and the desire for her stretched and grew inside him with every passing second. Darkness surrounded him. *More. More.*

He pulled her tighter into his embrace until the heat of her skin burned him as if no clothing existed between them. Whatever he'd thought he felt all those years ago was nothing compared to the desperation dominating his brain. The faint tremor underneath her skin fed the wild need for so much more. He was spiraling out of control.

When a small needy whimper sounded from her, his animal growled in response. The hunger for her erupted just below the surface as he struggled to remember what he'd been about to do before he kissed her. Sharp little claws from her hands busted through the thin fabric of his shirt and poked at his skin, an aggressive move that fueled the firestorm between them.

He savored her heat for a minute more before turning her body toward the door and forcing himself, in an act of sheer desperation and against his own will, to push her away and out the front door.

"Don't forget to tell my brother I said thanks but no thanks for the tease too. Okay, babe?"

"Why you—"

With that, he shut the door in her face and slammed the locks home. He gulped in some deep breaths, rested his forehead against the cool wood and did his best to deal with a racing heart. Everything in him wanted to open that door and drag her back inside. To show her what the real him inside really needed from her: rough, raw and animalistic. His body raged with the desperation of it. The shaking began in his hands and quickly raced through his extremities. Pain cramped his muscles, forcing him to his knees. But it was the howling in his head that drove him mad. Fuck. He deserved a fucking saint award for this. No man in his right mind would be able to resist the perfection of Cheyenne Ross.

"You bastard." The door did not muffle the sound of her voice or the anger rolling off her. But they would both be better off for this. At least she would. Five long years ago, he'd made his bed with her and now he suffered for it. Her arrival meant trouble for him with a capital T. If she didn't heed his warning and get the hell out of this town they'd both be sorry.

He pushed away from the door, his arms hung by his sides as if weighted down by lead. As for his brother... Whatever the problem, Kane was on his own. The elders had known exactly what was happening to Malcolm and had shown indifference. He still remained banished indefinitely. He wasn't about to return at their whim for another whipping or as a savior. They'd forced him to move on as best he could. Now they could too.

CHAPTER
TWO

hey stared at the dark wood door in front of her, still shocked that moments ago she'd been embroiled in a kiss the likes of which she'd never experienced and the next she stood out here in the cool night air as he disappeared into the interior of his house. His scent remained strong. Whether from her clothes or the fact he remained by the door she couldn't tell. She squeezed her eyes shut and breathed in deeply. Why would he wait for her? *Reject me once shame on you, reject me twice, shame on me.* Wasn't exactly how the old saying went but it sure felt appropriate.

He'd kissed her senseless and then slammed the door in her face. Other than the fact she still needed him to agree to return to clan land, she should be grateful.

Except for the first time in a very long time she felt alive. Not the automaton she'd become over the last year. Guilt sliced through her hot and swift.

You bastard!

He didn't care about her and she felt even less for him. If he thought a stupid kiss would scare her off he had another thing coming. Two could play at this game and she had plenty more tricks up her sleeve that did not involve his mouth, his hard muscled chest or the hard dick he'd been packing. Chey fingered the knife she'd holstered at her hip. Oh no. He didn't get to walk away again without a backward glance. If he did, he'd find her knife buried in it.

She glanced at the position of the moon in the sky and determined she had at least three hours before the sun came up and she wasn't about to spend that time prowling around outside his house. He'd gotten the best of her and she'd give him this round. But the fight had just gotten started. She wasn't about to lose now, not even against odds like this.

Looking down at the gravel footpath that led to his front door, Chey took a few steps backward. For tonight, her choice would be to try and take him by force and risk something bad happening, like them rolling around naked and sweaty on his bed. He'd pulled her tight against him and her body had fit perfectly against every heavily-muscled plane. She hadn't even bothered to fight him the slightest when he'd shoved his hand down her pants. Chey sighed at the memory.

Her sex still pulsed from that little taste of contact they'd shared. Never before or since had a man so thoroughly distracted her as to allow him to get the upper hand. Malcolm certainly presented himself as an intriguing opponent who offered her first real challenge in a very long time. She'd definitely keep at him even if it meant more time away from home.

Home... For a brief moment, she allowed the sadness to touch her as she jogged back to her car, knowing she shouldn't, that no good would come from reliving the past this time any more than it had in the past three hundred and sixty days.

She hopped into the Jeep she'd left in the trees out of sight and far enough away not to be heard and turned the key in the ignition. The smooth rumble of the engine drowned out some of the pain but not enough, so she flipped on the stereo too. *Focus Chey. Pull it back. You're on a mission with no time for self-pity so snap out of it.*

She thought of Malcolm and the energy that had fed between them. A phenomenon she'd only heard stories of and experienced once too many years ago to count. She no longer believed in a true bond mating, at least not for someone like her. If Malcolm was her mate then neither of them could have turned their back on the other. Something he'd clearly had no problem with and even she'd recovered after a few years. She'd moved on, started a new life, lost half of it again and now stood alone with desire burning between her legs and a job that had to be done.

Chey locked down those thoughts right alongside the pain and shoved it to the back for another day as she whipped a U-turn into the street. For now, she had some time to kill and a plan B to devise. Kane had warned her that Malcolm would give her a hard time, but he was counting on her to do what she did best and bring him home.

A serious storm brewed in their clan and threatened to spill over into other clans. The wolves had been keeping an eye on the floundering council of the were cougars and she feared they'd take action if it continued. Unfortunately, what lay between the cougars and the wolves were her kind, and everyone had grown restless and agitated. She hated to think what would happen if the Gunn brothers couldn't get things back under control. Unfortunately, Kane, as well as others, hypothesized it would take the unity of all three to stop the out of control spiral. She had to get Malcolm to go back.

The latest mating between Kane and his outsider had started off a chain reaction of mistrust that left the lonely Guardian on dangerous ground with his own council. With no death enforcers to watch his back, she figured there was a good chance he would be taken out unless Malcolm stepped in. But he had his own issues it would seem. Of all the Gunn brothers, the darkest rumors swirled around him. In the last year, she'd heard everything from his penchant for kinky sex to anger that raged out of control when someone pushed him too hard. He'd definitely changed from the almost *too* loyal clan guardian she'd met on a mission five years ago. Her brain puzzled over the changes but couldn't quite get a handle on them.

Chey shrugged. Malcolm's personal issues were not her problem. He'd made sure of that. All that mattered now was returning him to Kane so they could stop whatever or whoever had started this convoluted mess.

The cold predawn air twisted through Chey's hair as she turned a hard right into the Waffle House parking lot. She had to wait out Malcolm somewhere and this seemed as good a place as any. She needed to hurry up and get this job done so the knot in her stomach would ease and she could get away from the stirring of sexual need Malcolm had once again awakened in her.

Fuck! She couldn't stop obsessing over it. A hard sigh pushed through her lips while she swung herself from the Jeep onto the hard packed gravel of the parking lot. Like it or not, things changed every single day, sometimes more than she liked.

The bell above the door clanged loudly when she pulled the front door open and hustled into the warm air inside. The few employees and patrons all turned in her direction and stared openly. The subtle scents of curiosity and wariness wafted under her nose as she broke eye contact with the lone cook and hurried toward the empty booth in the corner.

The waitress approached and handed her a menu, which she didn't need. She already knew what she wanted and it wasn't going to be on the menu of any greasy diner.

"Can I get you something to drink?" The weariness in the woman's voice reminded Chey of the tough job she had in front of her. Malcolm would fight her every step of the way. It was up to her to find the method for keeping ahead of him.

"Coffee, black."

The waitress nodded and walked off.

Chey tilted her hip and reached for the cell phone inside her pants pocket when a familiar scent slammed into her. Another Cougar was sitting in the diner with her and it wasn't Malcolm.

She lifted her head and peered through her lashes as she scanned the room while pretending to check her messages on the phone. Only two other customers remained besides her. One sat on a stool at the counter and the other sat at a table at the opposite end of the building with his or possibly her back facing Chey's direction.

Not one to wait and see, she quickly rose to her feet and stalked to the other side of the diner to investigate. Sure enough, this time when she passed the man sitting at the counter, nausea roiled in her stomach at the stench coming from him. Cougar, sweat and fear. Not an attractive combination. How could she have missed him? Because she'd been too damned busy worrying about a dark haired man who wanted nothing to do with her instead of paying attention to her surroundings as usual. Not a good slip. Hunters had died for less.

A warning snarl pressed through her lips as the patron twisted on his stool.

"Take it easy, warrior. I'm only here to observe."

"Observe what exactly?" She didn't like the sound of this.

"Your mission."

"You're spying on me? Who the hell sent you? Kane? I swear, so help me, I am going to kick his ass." Her fists clenched at her side as red-hot anger grabbed hold of her. She'd been certain enough time had passed that her actions wouldn't be questioned or doubted. Apparently she'd been wrong.

"Whoa! Hold on. Just relax it's not that big of a deal."

"Not a big deal? Are you kidding me? I have never not completed a job I've been hired to do, and I sure as hell don't need a babysitter. So you can tell Kane he can go to—"

"Whoaaa." He held up his arms in mock surrender in a lame attempt to patronize her, which simply pissed her off more. She flexed the muscles of her forearms and her nails shifted and grew to claws. "Calm down, Cheyenne. We can't have you doing anything stupid in a public restaurant, now can we?"

"Then I suggest you go back to Kane and tell him that he can go fuck himself if this is the way it's going to be. I don't need this shit." She turned to head out the door and leave this shithole behind.

The man grabbed her by the elbow to stop her from leaving. A painful shudder crawled across her skin.

Automatically, she glared down at the golden skinned hand that dared to touch her. "You should—"

A loud, angry snarl sounded from behind her. Shivers raced up and down her spine, this time of an erotic nature. The hand holding her arm tightened around her skin. The idiot clearly didn't recognize a superior predator when he saw one.

"Carl, get your hands off her now if you want to live."

His eyes grew wide seconds before he dropped his hand back to his side. "Hello, Malcolm. Long time no see." Carl's voice dripped with sarcasm.

"Chey, go wait in the Jeep for me." At Malcolm's sharp toned demand, she whirled around to face him. Who he thought he was ordering her around like that she couldn't imagine, but when she opened her mouth to give him her opinion, she met his ice-cold gaze head on. Her heart stuttered in her chest at the rage and coldness she saw in the dark as night eyes that stared down Carl. It was no wonder the man was taking a step back.

She took a few steps away from Carl but didn't move to leave the diner; she wasn't about to leave Malcolm here like this. She knew that look, and if she left them alone there would be no one to stop him from a public attack. Then where would they all be if they ended up with two cougars trying to kill each other right here on the floor of the very public Waffle House?

"Why are you here, Carl?"

She watched the muscles bunch in Malcolm's neck and back as he spoke, a damn good indicator of just how close he was to losing it at any second. And that dumb ass Carl didn't even notice.

"I'm just here to observe."

"She's mine. Stay away from her."

Carl's eyebrows rose in surprise and she nearly choked herself. What the hell?

"You don't belong here." The venom in Malcolm's voice continued to ratchet higher. Goosebumps erupted along her bare arms.

"Well, neither do you. I hope you're at least maintaining your privacy in a place like this."

"Oh, like you are by following me here." At her voice, Malcolm turned and shot her a *you better quit talking now* look.

"Yeah whatever. I'm not here to harass your new bed buddy, Malcolm. I was just talking to her."

Malcolm took another step forward. "No, you were touching her." His voice lowered, sounding even more dangerous than before. "An act of aggression on my mate gives me certain rights, you know."

"Your mate?" She wouldn't keep quiet any longer. If she didn't cut him off at the knees now his possessive behavior would spiral out of control.

Malcolm ignored her and reached for Carl. He wrapped his hand around the other man's throat and squeezed. "If I see you near her again, I will kill you."

Carl grabbed at Malcolm's hand and fought to remove it from his skin, but Malcolm didn't budge. The pencil pusher Kane had sent to watch her was out matched and they all knew it.

"I'm here on official clan business. This outrageous behavior could get *you* killed." He croaked around the slight pressure Malcolm had on him.

"Malcolm, let's go." She stepped forward and pulled at his arm. That soft slide of skin touching was all it took for liquid heat to pool between her thighs, heat warming all of her long dormant womanly parts. What the hell was wrong with her? He stood in front of her behaving like a Neanderthal, yet the second she touched him, her only thoughts were of the kiss they'd shared earlier.

Malcolm's head swiveled sharply in her direction, his nose flared. He obviously noticed the change in her as well. Heat filled her cheeks as she sought something—anything—to look at that didn't include either of their knowing gazes. In a flash, Malcolm released Carl, took the one, long-legged step separating them to grab her arm and propelled her toward the door. Flames licked across her skin at the contact, her animal inside awakening for more.

Chey's breath caught in her throat, leaving her speechless and unable to stop him from taking her outside. He easily lifted her onto the passenger seat of her Jeep, his fingertips trailing along the length of her leg from hip to ankle. Despite the denim of her jeans acting as a barrier, she might as well have been naked. She looked down at the dark tanned skin of his hand as he touched her. Sudden fear of what this could mean paralyzed her. She refused to meet his eyes. Her body was out of control with a mind of its own.

He'd been right—she should have run. Now she feared it was too late.

"Go home, Malcolm. We're done." She prayed for once he'd listen.

"You think so do you?"

She swallowed, trying to force the lump from her throat. "We are. With Kane sending his lackey out here to check up on me, I'm pulling myself off this job. As far as I'm concerned, you're off the hook. If you choose to deal with him on your own that's on you. I don't play games or politics so your brother can kiss my ass."

"No, actually he can't. No one is ever going to touch you but me."

She jerked her head up and met his all too serious gaze. Shocked that he seemed to mean every last word.

"What's going on here?" She pushed at his hand on her thigh as it moved perilously close to the heated juncture between her legs. "You really need to stop touching me now."

"Why?" His hand skirted along her hip to the flat expanse of her belly, leaving a trail of heat and desire in its wake. When he was about to graze her breast, she gasped and pulled his hand away.

"I'm leaving." She wriggled away from him and threw her leg over the gearshift to switch seats. If he refused to stop then she'd take control and do what needed to be done, which right now was get as far away from Malcolm Gunn as possible before the animal inside her clawed its way out to reach him. Already, the cries in her head were out of hand and desperate. She'd been, unbelievably, about to push her hips into his hand when he'd moved around them instead.

Humiliation burned her cheeks as she considered that. It had just been too long, she tried to convince herself. That's all. About to plant her butt on the butter soft leather seat, Malcolm grabbed her around the waist and yanked her back down into the passenger chair where he proceeded to wrap and lock the seat belt across her thighs.

"What the fuck do you think you're doing?" Her lips curled into a snarl as her growing teeth poked at her lip. Shocked by the twin pricks of pain, she automatically looked down at her arms to see if any more of the change process had begun.

"Take a few deep breaths, darling, and relax. We're just going to talk until you can calm her down and lock her back inside." He glanced around the newly crowded parking lot. "Unfortunately this is not the place for us to lose control."

"I never lose control," she hissed.

"You will, darling, and very soon." He quickly brushed his lips across her jaw before jumping out of her reach.

Everything he did and said incited the anger and need building inside her. Fortunately, at least a small section of her brain still worked properly enough to keep her mouth shut and her breathing even. It was her only hope of regaining control. With this level of sexual lust coursing through her, the slightest tussle with any emotion would do nothing but fan the flames and leave her a writhing mess. Then where would she be?

Fucking the most gorgeous man I've ever had the pleasure to hate in the middle of the parking lot of a flipping Waffle House, that's where.

Chey pressed her lips together to suppress a groan. The last thing she needed to do was get involved with trouble, good looking or not. She ground her back teeth together when he hopped into the driver's side and held his hand out for the keys. At this point, she and the cougar wanted to fight. Maybe they had different goals in mind but they were both frustrated and he was a great target. Chey resisted and dug into her pants' pocket to fish out the keys. He slid them into the ignition and cranked her baby up, letting the engine warm for just a minute before throwing it into gear and hauling out of the parking lot.

From the corner of her eye, she caught movement at the far edge of the building. The anger inside boiled higher. Carl had been watching them. Malcolm had recognized him immediately, and apparently not a lot of love was lost between them.

"Do you know him?"

The muscle in Malcolm's jaw twitched and his lips pressed together in a grim line. Looked like her guess was right.

"Yeah, we grew up together in the clan, but we had a falling out a while back. I could have done without seeing him again."

"I still can't believe Kane sent the likes of *him* to follow me. A pansy ass cougar like him gives me the creeps. Why send someone who doesn't even possess the balls to stand up to either one of us?"

"Kane didn't send him here, and I better not see you and him anywhere near each other again." His threat came on the wave of a low growl.

Chey pressed the palm of her hand to her forehead as the headache he'd been giving her since he showed up flared to an all-new high. "Your attitude is getting old, Malcolm." She let her head fall back onto the headrest and slid her eyes closed. "Good thing I'm going home just as soon as I drop you off," she muttered under her breath. An extra burst of tension radiated from him and she bit her tongue to keep from smiling. Why she wanted to poke him so bad she didn't understand, but a childish satisfaction settled over her.

Now if her body would stop vibrating with sexual desire, she could go home and forget about him.

"Wait." She sat up in her seat. "What do you mean Kane didn't send him? How do you know what he said?"

"Oh, I heard what the little prick said. Trust me. If Kane wanted you or I checked up on he would never send Carl. He's an untrustworthy snake in the grass who is only out for himself."

The venom in Malcolm's words startled her. "But if Kane didn't send him then what is he doing here?" Confusion clouded her thoughts as she tried to understand.

"Finally she asks the right question."

CHAPTER
THREE

On the drive back to Malcolm's house at the edge of the Nantahala national forest, Chey's skin crawled from doing nothing. She desperately wanted to glare at him, yell at him—hell, even jumping from the Jeep and disappearing into the early morning light just peeking over the horizon sounded good.

Arousal, anger and guilt were not a good combination and she needed some time to clear her head. It was the arousal more than anything that puzzled her. Her body burned for a man that was, for all intents and purposes, a criminal. The profile she'd compiled on him over the years spoke of a rebellious but loyal teenager who'd worshipped his mother. After she died, things began to change. For one, he'd met her.

ELIZA GAYLE

Unfortunately, she remembered the day as clearly as if it had been yesterday, not five years ago.

She'd crossed over into his clan's territory on a dare and he'd hunted her. From the moment she'd scented him something shifted inside her. His presence tugged continuously at her mind. However, fear of a black cougar had practically been bred in her so she raced back to the neutral zone where she belonged. That first day she'd not seen him, but she'd known he watched her from somewhere close by. His scent enthralled her.

Chey'd returned every single night, playing chicken with a Death Enforcer. Until one night, he'd decided to capture her. He'd gone from cougar to man in an instant, pouncing on her before she even blinked. Every cell in her body had lit up that night and she'd been prepared to take him as her first. They'd wrestled and fought, scratched and bit until finally Malcolm pinned her to the ground belly down.

He'd entered her from behind in one dark, fast and thrilling thrust that made her scream from the glorious pain and pleasure. Their cries of passion and lust filled the night air until they were both lost in the frenzy. Then he'd frozen above her. He'd scrambled to his feet spewing insults she'd never expected from the man she'd inexplicably trusted. He shifted back to the sleek cougar she'd been awed by and disappeared into the woods.

Left confused and hurt, she'd curled into a ball and wept. She'd lost her innocence and ability to trust that night and all she heard in her head over and over were his parting words.

Not in this lifetime or any other would he mate with a half-breed.

Chey turned her face into the wind and let the rough air wipe away the tears dripping on her cheeks. Why she would shed a tear for him after all this time and not the family she'd so recently lost angered her. He deserved less than nothing from her.

The first year after that night was unbearable for her. Rumors of Malcolm's quick descent from exalted enforcer to troublemaker filtered through to the neutral zone. Out of some sick fascination, she'd written down every scrap of information about him she could find. By the time the stories of dark magic and even darker sex made their way to her family, Malcolm had been outcast. Stripped of his rank and torn from his family as punishment for his outrageous behavior. Apparently his clan had no use for a man who couldn't play by the rules. He'd become exactly what he'd feared that fateful night.

When the stories of his sexual conquests came pouring in, she'd locked away his file and moved on. Yet, he'd been like a magnet she couldn't resist when the request from Kane came down. A year ago, her world had turned upside down and she no longer cared what anyone thought of her. Especially not Malcolm. Unfortunately for her, the sexual attraction she'd felt all those years ago had not died. Why did an irresponsible, demanding and often cruel man excite her? Couldn't she ever do anything the easy way? He stood for everything she never wanted in her life again.

The crunching of the gravel under the tires as he swerved from the highway caught her attention and she opened her eyes to see where they were. His place again. She recognized the unpaved road and the already familiar scent. Or was that just the man sitting next to her?

When they rounded the final bend, his small cabin came into view in front of her. Things looked different in the light of day, starting with the little shack across from his home that said *Park Station* in black letters across the top of the building.

"You're a park ranger?" Her voice quivered in shock. Not in her wildest dreams did she expect this.

"Don't sound so surprised. What did you think I was?" He glanced over at her with hard, assessing eyes waiting for her answer.

"I don't know what I expected, but it sure as hell wasn't this." She gestured to the ranger station.

"I'm surprised you missed it last night. But don't worry your pretty little head, darling. I have no intention of shattering your illusions of what a bastard I am. I'm not a park ranger or at least not permanently. A friend of mine had an emergency out west and asked if I could stay at his place and fill in for a couple of months until he got things straightened out and could get back."

Chey wasn't sure what shocked her more. The fact that he had a friend or that he would actually help one out. His huge attitude rubbed her all kinds of wrong but now she felt a little ashamed that just the fact that he'd help out a friend was more than she'd expected from him. She really didn't even know him, other than the spotty details of a misspent youth, the trouble he'd caused for his brother months ago and the heat burning just under her skin, aching—wanting.

Malcolm threw the Jeep into first and popped the clutch to park them right in front of his door.

"Guess I'll be leaving now." She hesitated, unsure. Despite her memories, she sensed something different about him. "If your brother wants you back, he can come and get you himself." She unfastened the belt and moved to get out of the vehicle.

"The only place you're going is inside with me. We have a situation to straighten out."

Chey rolled her eyes. "What is there to straighten out? I'm letting you off the hook—at least until your brother sends someone else."

He snorted. "Letting me off the hook? I don't think so Chey. You know as well as I do there is a lot more going on than simply a job. I warned you not to come near me again and you didn't listen. Now I can't get your taste out of my mind for even a second and my dick has been hard since the second I scented you in my house." He pressed his hand against the hard bulge in his jeans and stroked downward, a move she couldn't take her eyes from. "This is not business as usual."

Her tongue poked out and moistened her parched lips, her brain already losing focus as he continued to touch himself. Liquid pooled between her thighs and her nipples tightened painfully against her shirt. She looked up and met his gaze, not missing the change of his deep blue eyes to nearly black. Not to mention he stared at her like he planned to devour her.

She gulped at the stern lines of his face, the stark desire evident in the firm set of his jaw and fierce expression in his eyes. He wasn't going to let her just walk away and she wasn't sure she could fight that kind of determination. If she dug deep into her own psyche, she'd known this would happen and she'd chosen to come anyway.

"It's just lust, Malcolm. I know you're familiar with the concept. You're a healthy, good-looking male and I'm a female who hasn't had sex in far longer than is healthy for my breed. This *is* normal."

"Then you won't mind going inside to prove that." He pulled her from her seat, pressing her against his big, hard body. The softer curves of her figure fit snug against the firm muscles of his chest and stomach. She melted against him. Want churned in her belly, along with need tinged with desperation. The heat of his touch burned through her clothes, setting off sparks of pure pleasure across her skin. He wrapped his hands around her waist as he turned and carried her from the Jeep.

"Wrap your legs around my waist, Chey." His tone had changed. It was still demanding but delivered with a husky undertone of ragged need. She hid her smile when she buried her face in his neck. It felt incredibly satisfying and less scary knowing he struggled as well.

His hands slid to her bottom and his strength infused through her clothing, leaving her with a racing heart and a pulsing body. Would it really be that bad if she indulged just this once? Something about the dominant way he treated her had gotten under her skin and she definitely needed more. One day. If he didn't have anything else to do today, then they could spend the day in his warm bed, naked, having mind-blowing sex they both seemed to want.

She'd about convinced herself a no strings day of sex would be just what they needed when he stepped them through the front door and pushed her against the wall, his hips grinding into the soft denim covered flesh between her thighs.

A low moan sounded in her throat at the contact. His stiff erection pressed right up against... "Oohhh." She pulsed and swelled when he applied pressure in just the right spot. She wriggled her hips against him feeling the long awaited pleasure she'd held out from for so long.

Malcolm pushed her harder against the wall, effectively stilling her hips. "Not yet, baby. Not until I'm inside you. I want to feel every pulse and stroke of your hot pussy wrapped around my dick when you come," he growled into her ear.

Whimpers and incoherent babble fell from her lips as she clawed at his shirt, shredding it and sending strips of cloth flying around the room. With her hands on his bare skin, she reached for one of his flat, brown nipples and slowly scraped over it with a claw, leaving a red mark behind.

"Little hellcat, aren't you?" He ground his hips almost painfully against hers, ratcheting up the heat and need flaring between them. "That's okay because you're my hellcat from now on and I better not ever see you allowing a man to lay hands on you or so help me I will kill him. No questions asked."

She snarled at his words, digging the sharp tips of her claws into the taut flesh over his pecs. Her animal burst free. There would be no tempering her and *she* loved the possessiveness of his demands. Couldn't get enough of them.

He let go of her ass and pushed her legs to the floor until she stood on her own two very shaky limbs. With smooth, practiced moves, he had her pants undone and down around her ankles before she could blink an eye.

"Lift." She obeyed, raising her feet one at a time from the confinement of her jeans. When she stood only in her tiny black panties and top, he got down on his knees so that his face was even with her heated pussy.

Her heart pounded so fast she heard nothing but its frantic beat. With his sharp teeth, he grabbed at the thin fabric protecting her and ripped it from her body, his nose flaring when he caught her scent.

Seconds later, hot air brushed across her folds and then paused. Waiting. Each second of anticipation drove her closer to crazy. "Malcolm, please." Her voice shook with each word. Not that she cared. All that mattered was getting him inside her, filling her, fucking her.

"When I say so, Chey. That's something you'll have to learn. Although I enjoy the begging, baby, so feel free, but don't expect to always get what you want." His hands nudged her legs apart before his fingers explored her slick outer lips. "Damn woman, are you always this wet or is this just for me?"

A strangled cry fell from her lips when a thumb glanced across her sensitive nub. "Oh, and very responsive too... You and I are going to have so much fun." He laughed. "Are you ready, Chey?"

She bit her lip and nodded, looking down in time to watch his tongue spear her sex, sliding through the folds and lapping at the moisture he'd created by just touching her. Her hands grasped for something to hold onto, finally latching onto his thick, wavy hair. She shot from the wall when he pressed his hot tongue to her, the sensation more than she could bear.

Malcolm's fingers and tongue fell away and she wanted to cry. Tears sprang to her eyes as he stood to his full height just a couple of inches above her own. Arms shot out and captured her around the waist, pulling her close before lifting her again with his palms planted firmly on her ass for balance. This time she didn't need to be told to wrap her legs around him; she instinctively knew what he wanted. Her feet locked around him left her open and settled in just the right position where his cock nudged against her wetness.

Chey wrapped her hands around Malcolm's neck, loving the smooth skin with a baby fine layer of hair that rubbed against her like silk. Magnetically drawn to his mouth, she slipped her tongue through his lips to explore and devour. Her mind opened to every sensation and tingle he created with the touch of his tongue, his hands and especially his erection pushing slowly through her folds. Her breath caught in her throat as he stretched her, almost to the point where she wasn't sure if she could take him.

She'd remembered him as well endowed but damn sure didn't remember him this big—this hard. Fissures of excitement skated up her spine, making her head tingle. She kissed him harder until she thought she might lose her mind waiting for him to enter her fully. It had been so long since she'd felt like this, and, to her shame, more than a little part of her was delighted to feel excited again. Later she might have to pull her guilt out and reexamine it—but not now. Now she focused on the swollen tip of Malcolm stroking her, on the verge of taking her.

CHEY'S TONGUE stroked his mouth with short quick bursts that heated his blood and sent his mind careening with pleasure. He held his body rigid while he struggled to maintain control. But God help him, touching her naked skin and tasting her delicious flesh had been his undoing. The more she struggled against him, the harder his animal fought to break free, but he wouldn't be gentle or slow. Not with the heat of her core sucking at his dick and her sweet little mouth devouring him like a starved woman.

Sharp canines sank into his bottom lip and her tongue swiped at the drops of blood she'd produced. The sweet and coppery scent along with her reaction to it broke the animal free. He pressed her body tight against the wall and slammed into her snug channel, burying himself to the hilt. She tore her mouth from his and let loose a wail of pleasure that would carry for miles. The lush, sensual sound like music to his ears.

He hoped every creature known to mankind heard her. Nothing would please him more than to declare to everyone he'd claimed his mate.

Malcolm's blood boiled. He picked up speed as he thrust into her, each time adding a little more force. The snug fit felt like a tight fist squeezing him, driving him wild, as did the knowledge of a perfect fit when he was inside her. He didn't know how he would get enough of her. He'd been the worst kind of fool to walk away from her all those years ago. She was perfection in every way. Her bloodline meant nothing in the face of what having a mate meant to him. For once in his life, he actually wanted to stay with a woman. To know her. To love her. The reality of his life had meant nothing since that day in the woods. Nothing. Now, after all this time he'd finally realized where he belonged...with her, in her.

Heat rose between them as their skin slickened with sweat and the pleasure riding them both. He buried his face in her neck and scraped his teeth against the thin, soft skin of her shoulder. He inhaled deeply, letting the unique scent of her fill him. His cock swelled until he thought he would explode from the flames licking over every inch of his body. She gasped and thrashed against him, forcing him to push his hips against her to create an increased pressure where she needed it most. His mate was about to have an orgasm and she didn't want him to stop. His heart stuttered at the image; her losing control in his arms and giving herself to him unconditionally was more than he'd ever hoped for.

The hard buds of her nipples poked at his chest as he continued to piston into her, driving them both into a frenzy of lust and feral need. The time for soft words or expressions had escaped him as the wild hunger for his mate propelled him to the edge, threatening his very sanity.

"You're mine now," he growled, cringing at the feral sound of his own voice. Her lips parted on another long moan as her muscles clenched around him, coating him with her cream. His breath hitched, stuck in his chest. He couldn't breathe through something this good and it was so fucking good.

"Oh God, Malcolm, what are you doing to me?" Her hands twined in his hair tugging and pulling as she came while the shudders racked her body.

"I'm loving you, baby. Something I should have done a long time ago. So get used to it because you belong to me now." Never had a woman shredded his control like this. The cougar had her now but the man wanted his mate just as much. He'd just never known it. As each thrust threatened to send him shooting over the edge, he knew he never wanted this to end. Soon she would become his world and own him as much as he owned her. Two would become one and neither of them would ever be alone again.

A fresh wave of heat rushed to his groin as his balls tightened against his body. He couldn't hold back from her any longer, and he pushed harder, faster, his fingers digging into her buttocks until the orgasm ripped through him, sending him headlong into an abyss as he unwittingly gave her everything that he had. His body, his heart and his cum.

She screamed out his name again as she, too, catapulted into another release that had her tightening around him, dragging every bit of pleasure from his body until finally he stilled against her, wrung out from the best goddamn sex he'd ever experienced in his life. He couldn't imagine how he would survive when they took things slow and easy, drawing more from her during a session designed to get into her head and her secret desires hidden underneath the surface. Or when he explored her submissive side. The scent of it was subtle, but he'd draw it out. Teach her the exquisite pleasure of submitting to her mate. She would be his pride and joy, he just knew it.

She stirred against him and he raised his head from her shoulder, meeting her gaze. She definitely had the look of a woman well sated but the tinge of sadness around the edges was impossible to miss.

"Chey, did I hurt you?" She curled in her bottom lip and shook her head. Her denial seemed hollow when he spied the sheen of tears pooling in her eyes. He gently eased his hips back and slid from her body so he could move them. Guilt hammered at him for letting the animal steal away his control. He'd never allowed that to happen, but with her, all bets were off. Everything changed.

He gently curled his arm around her bottom and lifted her back into his arms, loving the sensation of more warm skin brushing against his abdomen. Worry unfurled when she turned her head away from him, avoiding anymore eye contact. Stopping in front of the couch, he placed her on the soft cushions and grabbed the blanket he kept draped across the back to cover her.

"Bathroom," she whispered.

"It's just down the hall there." He pointed toward his bedroom where she'd been standing not all that long ago trying to trap him. Chey's feet hit the floor and she padded quietly toward his room, gathering up her clothes as she went. Her quiet, careful demeanor worried him yet didn't stop him from getting excited when she bent over to pick up her pants. The woman had one fine ass.

After she disappeared, he heard the door close and the distinct click of the lock. Something akin to fear shivered down his spine. What had he missed? He paced over to the door, grabbed up his jeans and shoved his legs in them. Frustration made him nervous. He needed her to accept him for who he really was but he should have held back, been gentle, taken a little more time with her.

Fucking dumb ass.

"I should probably get going." He whirled at the sound of her voice, shocked that she continued to sneak up on him.

"Look, Chey, I know—"

"Don't, Malcolm. Everything is fine. I'll admit that I got a little emotional there at the end but that's my own fault. It's just been a long time since... " she hesitated. "Well, since I've had sex."

He smiled at her. He couldn't help it, she looked so beautiful and vulnerable standing there trying to explain herself. "I understand, Chey. I think what we are both feeling is a little overwhelming."

She winced when he spoke those words and the hair on the back of his neck stood up. Her hesitancy spoke volumes.

"It was just sex. Very good sex, but still... It's time for me to go home. In fact, I should have never accepted this assignment."

He lowered his voice, doing his best to control the temper rising. "This was way more than sex and you know it, and no, you aren't going anywhere."

She stared at him for a long moment, her eyes changing from soft regret to shock before he saw resignation finally set in. She knew exactly what was going on between them and no one would be foolish enough to think walking away would be simple. They'd both suffer for it.

"I can't stay here. You don't understand."

"I understand all I need to. You're my mate in every way and a nature like that is impossible to fight. I made the worst possible mistake a man can make five years ago, but I intend to spend the rest of my life making up for it."

Her shoulders sagged. "That's what you think? That this is simply mating heat and that we have no say so in the course of our lives?"

"I'm thinking I'm damn grateful this has happened. It's probably more than I could ever deserve but nonetheless, I won't be letting go."

"I'm not your mate, Malcolm."

"That's bullshit and we both know it. Nothing like this has ever happened to me before and I damn well know what mating heat looks like."

She shook her head and closed her eyes. "It's impossible. I can't be your mate."

"Why the hell not?"

She hesitated and stark fear glittered in her eyes. "Because I'm already mated."

Everything in Malcolm's body froze as her words whiplashed through his brain. As he processed the implications of what she said, he was certain he'd not heard her right.

"What the hell did you say?"

"Please, Malcolm, you heard me. Don't make me repeat them."

An enraged snarl left his lips, causing her to take two steps back, pissing him off further. No way. This fucking could not be happening.

He grabbed her arm and whipped her around, shoving her hair to the side so he could get a look at the back of her neck. There was only one way to know for sure. The blood drained from his head when he spied the small scar at the back of her neck. Where his mark should have been, someone else had claimed her. She'd forsaken him for another. Allowed another man to bite her. The cougar raged inside of him as he gritted his teeth to control it. Fire burned in his veins. Despite everything, the animal demanded freedom; he would steal what belonged to another.

Pain ripped through his guts straight to his heart. He stumbled away from her, the claws in his hand shredding his skin. He'd known better than to believe. Nothing good ever came from giving trust. *Ever.* Now they would all suffer.

"Get out!" he snapped.

He shoved her in the general direction of the door and stalked to the back of the house and his escape. He had to face the truth. He'd seen the evidence with his own eyes, but if he didn't get away from her and her scent, the cougar would force his will on them both.

CHAPTER
FOUR

Tears welled and spilled onto Chey's cheeks as her legs gave out and she sank to the ground. The pain and rage that had burned from Malcolm when she'd blurted out the truth would likely haunt her for a long time, not to mention her own remorse at the mess she'd managed to create. What had started out as a quick meeting of warm bodies and similar needs had quickly morphed into something far more complicated that neither of them was ready for.

What had happened? Chey couldn't remember a time in her life, not even with John, where she'd been so overwhelmed that all of her carefully crafted control had flown out the window. She'd wanted to explain it away as akin to a dam breaking after a long time of no sexual contact, but no, she'd been a fool. Even if her mixed blood had created an abnormally high sex drive, even for cougars, she'd never gotten mindless over it ever before. Five years ago, she'd sworn Malcolm was different, but when the physical pain of loss eventually subsided, she'd convinced herself it had been of her own making.

Chey placed her hands on the hard wood floor and pushed herself up. She couldn't sit here fighting the tears all day long. She stared at the wall that just a little while ago Malcolm had used to take her in the most demanding and urgent sex she'd ever experienced. It had been more than sex but she wasn't about to admit it to him. She had a life to return to, even if that meant more pain and guilt. They'd both become her security blanket.

Now she needed to get as far away from here as fast as she could, but her feet didn't want to move. The blinding pain in Malcolm's gaze threatened to keep her on her knees. She needed to explain the rest of her story to him. Make him understand the situation wasn't quite as bad as she'd watched him leap to. Although where she would get the words to explain what had happened to her mate and her involvement in it, she had no idea. Fuck it. She didn't need forgiveness from him.

Even her family hadn't succeeded in getting her to talk about it and it wasn't for the lack of trying, that was for sure. Renewed grief slashed at her mind as she saw the final look in John's eyes, the love and trust that he'd wanted her to remember. She glanced around the room needing... *dying* for air. Outside. Her brain attempted to function. Standing in Malcolm's house after he'd ordered her out made her uneasy. She slipped on her soft leather moccasins and headed for the door. She could wait for him to return in her Jeep. Somehow it seemed less intrusive.

With one last glance behind her, she twisted the knob and pulled the door open. The scent of blood slammed into her like a ton of bricks, the smell so strong she knew it meant there would be a lot of blood. Fear stabbed at her heart as her mind leapt to Malcolm. *Oh Goddess, no please. Don't let it be him. Not again...please.*

She forced her head to tilt down and immediately nausea roiled through her body and dry heaves gripped her stomach. Limbs dangled from a shredded body, nearly every inch of skin peeled away. Jagged claw marks covered what little was left and the throat had so clearly been ripped from the neck with razor sharp teeth. The face, however, had not been touched: the thin lips, slightly parted; crooked little nose probably from being broken so many times; and dead blank eyes staring out from the lifeless body.

"What the fuck?" Her head jerked up in time to see Malcolm running from behind her Jeep, skidding to a stop on the opposite side of the body. "What did you do?" He looked up at her with hard, questioning eyes.

"Me?" she uttered in shock. "You think I did this? That I am capable of—" She shuddered.

"I don't know what you're capable of."

She winced at the ice in his tone that chilled her, all the way to the bone. Bile rose in her throat under the constant onslaught of the blood and gore scents filling the air. In a hunt, this kind of thing never bothered her but seeing one of her own kind gutted and flayed out in front of her was a completely different story.

She turned away, unable to look anymore when Malcolm grabbed her elbow and yanked her around. "Not so fast. You didn't answer my question. What happened? Did Carl show up after I left and you get into it again with him?"

She looked at him with sheer incredulity; he still thought she did this. Chey yanked her arm from his grasp and hissed at him. "I found him like this, so you don't have to be an asshole. Hell, you were outside before me. How do I know you didn't do this?"

"That's just ridiculous. Carl was a jerk, but after your little revelation in there I didn't even have a reason to be angry with him anymore. You'll clearly let any man touch you."

Chey gasped. "Why you son of a—"

"Careful, Chey. Your bitch is showing."

She gritted her teeth, grinding them together to hold her tongue. This situation required a clear head and a plan. Something neither of them would find if they kept sniping at each other. Despite the calm and cold exterior he presented her with, she knew better. She'd experienced firsthand the heat raging within him and no way had he reined that in in such a short amount of time. That very rage vibrated in the energy around them, barely restrained, no matter what he claimed. Although the violent energy around the body made her uncertain of everything she sensed.

"There's a lot of pain and anger out here. It's hard to sift through." The negative waves swamped her was more like it. Her head pounded along with them.

"That's pretty obvious ... Wait, you can feel it? You're an empath?" He shoved his hands in his pockets and settled his gaze on her face, looking and waiting.

"Yes, somewhat. All of my family is, in one way or another. Being a *half-breed* does have its perks." She couldn't resist the barb. They normally called themselves hybrids but he'd become insistent on the half-breed term. He'd definitely burrowed under her skin and she couldn't shake it.

Precious seconds ticked by as he continued to stare at her, as if searching for some mysterious answer. "Who are you then?"

"What the hell is that supposed to mean? You've been calling me a half-breed for half a decade in case you've forgotten because I sure as hell haven't. Although in some circles my bloodline is considered an asset."

Malcolm snorted. "Yeah, the circles who hire killers."

"Fuck you."

"No thanks; you already did."

Chey's head pounded. Pain whipped through every cell of her body at the reminder of what she'd become. Not a killer but that didn't absolve the blood on her hands. She grabbed her head and slid to her knees. Violence swirled around her. Her body was in overload mode and couldn't take much more before shutting down.

"What's going on?" The mistrust in Malcolm's question turned her stomach.

"Just fucking give me a minute and leave me alone."

Thankfully he shut his mouth. Blood thundered in her ears as the anxiety rose to a dangerous level. She needed to distract herself and damned quick. Malcolm paced around the body that lay between them and moved closer. Involuntarily, she recoiled. To her he looked every inch the predator she knew him to be, stalking his prey. If he did this she needed to get away *now*. Chey had no intention of getting trapped in his claws.

"How come you smell more like cougar than wolf? It took me a while when I first started hunting you to even figure it out. You're different than the others. How?"

She stumbled over something on the ground but was afraid to look down sure it would be a loose foot or worse. "Stop this. There's a dead body lying at your front door and you are questioning me? Stop looking for trouble where there is none. It's ridiculous."

"Ridiculous why? I left you in the house, told you to leave and I come back to this, you standing over a dead cougar's body."

"Oh for Pete's sake. You left me for what? All of five minutes?"

"Try at least twenty. And this kill is easily that fresh."

"Which makes you as much of a suspect as me."

"Except one thing." He paused and she waited. "Neither one of us has a drop of blood on them."

She narrowed her eyes and contemplated his suggestion while she sought out his energy. There wasn't much. Somehow he shielded from her. "You must be familiar with an empath's ability. You're quite adept at shielding from it."

"Is that what I'm doing?" His hand raked through his unruly hair. "I'm just standing here waiting for you to say something. Maybe you should take a break from your woo woo stuff and just tell me what you saw." He took another step forward until he was close enough that either of them could have reached for the other, except they didn't. Instead, the virtual distance between them grew as he eyed her suspiciously. What exactly had he done after he'd left her in such a rage? She'd never witnessed a more angry man and changing clothes at his own house would not be difficult. No, Malcolm couldn't talk his way out of this one yet.

She kept quiet. He made it crystal clear that whatever she said wasn't going to make a difference. For now they were at an impasse. Chey averted her eyes from Malcolm and glanced at the issue at hand. She couldn't wish this mess away now. They were going to have to work together to deal with this one. A cougar death normally brought out an investigation team and the damn council would be hopping to get involved when they found out about it.

She tipped her head and met Malcolm's gaze. The fierce intensity she recognized made her want to squirm, something she managed to resist with every fiber of her pride. His attempts at intimidation only annoyed her, making her want to poke at him. Unfortunately, the image of pain flashing in his eyes when she'd told him about John gnawed relentlessly at her guilt, giving her no peace at all. She somehow felt obligated to tell him the rest, dissuade his anger a little, but damn it, those were her private thoughts that she wasn't ready to share with him or anyone else for that matter.

So why did she want to reach for him? The arms he crossed aggressively over his chest should be wrapped around her as he kissed her and held on to her. She imagined the light hair sprinkled across his arm sliding against her soft and silky until she purred for him. Chey grabbed her head and dropped her gaze. She couldn't keep looking and thinking of him like that or she'd be launching her body against his, begging his forgiveness for everything she'd said. Her temples pounded as her thoughts ran rampantly through her mind, not letting up for a second.

She had to move away from the body and its violent energy before the pain in her head worsened. Her reasoning sounded hollow even to her because it wasn't the murder that held her under a firestorm of emotions. No, that honor belonged to the unscrupulous black haired devil standing in front of her, not letting her go.

Fingers snapped in front of her face bringing her back from her thoughts. "Chey, where'd ya go?" She blinked at him before realizing that she'd been so lost in her own head she hadn't heard a word he'd said.

"I'm sorry, what did you say?"

He frowned down at her, impatience crossing his face. "This is a serious situation we've got here. Do you think you could pay attention for a few minutes?" The biting words snapped from his mouth caused her to cringe. His constant desire to be in control of their situation bristled against her own struggle to make sense of the mess.

"I know you're frustrated and you're not alone in that but snapping at me isn't going to get us anywhere. We need to work together on this." She moved away from Malcolm then, hoping to ease both their need. The smell of sex clung to their skins, and, despite his anger and pain, or maybe because of it, along with her feeling some of the same, their animals were drawn and still attracted.

Maybe the best thing she could do for the both of them at this point would be to leave. That had been her plan all along so why not? She could contact Kane from the road and let him know what happened. Hiding this would be impossible. Better to get a cleaner in here as quickly as possible. If she ended up a suspect, her own family would send an investigator. It was customary.

"Where do you think you're going?" Once again, she'd gotten caught up in her mind, swamped with a range of emotion and violence she could barely think through. She looked down to see her hand resting on the warm metal of her Jeep. Her protective instincts had told her to flee and that's what she'd been about to do.

"I think I should leave." In the blink of an eye he was behind her, pressing his body against hers, heat flaming between them.

"I don't think so. Not until I have some answers and we get this mess cleaned up. Before you showed up, things were smooth and calm. Now they've gone to shit. You aren't just walking away."

"Then I'd better make a phone call." She didn't bother to argue. Fatigue was setting in.

"Going to tell him what you did? Or will you try to hide the fact you fucked another man?" A rough hand grabbed her arm from the door and yanked it behind her back, pinning her in place.

Her body went rigid at the vicious, pain-filled tone of his voice. He thought she wanted to call her mate. Chey exhaled a slow breath, calming her racing heart as she relaxed her body against his. She refused to be baited. Now it was his turn to go rigid as the muscles rippled and hardened under his skin and pressed against her back.

"It's not what you think, I need to explain—"

"Don't. It is what it is but until we figure this out you're not leaving my sight." Chey's eyes slid closed as she blocked out the bad and focused on the delicious good that he created every time he touched her. Touching Malcolm anymore was *so* not a good idea, but with her arm locked behind her back and his mouth just above her ear, she couldn't think straight. Thank Goddess the overpowering stench of coagulating blood and an already decaying body reminded her of the trouble they faced. As far as she knew, she could very well be in the arms of a murderer. He'd been alone just as long as her and would be considered a suspect as well.

She'd read his file and knew for a fact that he could be a cold-hearted bastard when he wanted to be. He'd proven again and again he could be a ruthless man when he thought the end result justified the means. And so far, he'd narrowly escaped imprisonment or worse. His status as a black cougar saved him more than once, a fact that burned her up. Just because a person was lucky by birth shouldn't excuse all the bad things they did.

Then she'd foolishly agreed to this mission and her world turned upside down. Again.

Memories of him taking her there in his house up against the wall assaulted her. The encounter had been more brutal and delicious than anything she'd experienced, even with John. More vicious guilt stabbed through her head. No matter how much the experience affected either of them, the memory of her dead husband haunted her. Whatever this violent need between her and Malcolm meant, it had to stop. She couldn't go back there.

"Do you think you can really stop me if I want to leave?" She gritted out the words.

"You don't want to test me like that, you won't like the results. But to answer your question, yes if I decide you can't leave then you won't."

His words left no room for compromise and part of her liked the fact that he had that much confidence.

"Pretty arrogant for a man who thinks I just killed and gutted another of our kind. What makes you so sure you would be safe?"

"I can handle it."

"You have no idea what you're dealing with, do you? I'm not some ordinary female you can just order around at your whim. Just because I let you dominate me a little during sex, doesn't mean shit in a situation like this. I *can* take care of myself."

His voice lowered at her ear. "So tell me then... What am I dealing with?"

Chey was tired of trying to explain herself. The man couldn't be any more arrogant if he tried so she would just have to show him. Make him understand exactly what he was dealing with.

She relaxed, letting the tension ease from her body as the familiar burn rushed across her skin. White fur covered her arms and hands and the features of her body shifted only as far as she would allow them.

Malcolm's hands dropped away from her and he stepped back, leaving her to catch herself against the

Jeep to prevent from falling to the ground. "What the hell?"

She turned her head and met his gaze head on, watching his eyes widen at the sight of what she knew to be opaque blue eyes, surrounded by a thin bright white coat of hair. Wolf's eyes. She stopped the change there and waited for his next reaction.

"You're a—" He snapped his mouth shut, not finishing his sentence.

"What? An anomaly? A freak? Or why not go all out for the abomination, everyone else does." Chey closed her eyes and visualized the fur gone and replaced by the pale skin of the human until she was certain it was done. She'd made her point; there was no reason to prolong it. It was more than wolf's blood she carried. She could also shift at will between her two animals.

She fished into the pocket of her jeans and pulled out her cell phone, punching in the number before holding it up to her ear. Malcolm stood speechless two feet away while the phone at the other end began to ring in her ear. The heavy weight of disappointment at his reaction pounded in her head taking up residence with the residual violence of the scene. She really needed to get away from here.

"Hello."

"We have a problem." She heard the sigh at the other end and hoped he was in a good mood. She and Malcolm were likely going to need his support.

"Tell me."

"The man you sent to follow me is dead. I found him at Malcolm's doorstep this morning."

"What man? I didn't send anyone else but you. Are we dealing with a human casualty?"

"He said you sent him. And no, he's a cougar plus."

Silence.

"I thought you found him dead? How did he say who sent him?" Chey ground her teeth together in frustration. Kane sounded genuinely surprised; it was obvious in his voice pattern.

"I ran into him a few hours ago. We had words then Malcolm interrupted and they had words."

"And by words I don't imagine you mean a friendly chat?"

"What do you think? The idea of someone following me to make sure I did my job pissed me off."

"I didn't send anyone. I knew if anyone could get him back here it would be you. Fucking A, Chey!"

Realization slammed into her. She'd known exactly what he thought made her uniquely qualified for this job and he'd set her up for a reason. Hell, anyone with a tranq gun could probably have grabbed Malcolm and possibly even avoided this new mess. "Well, whoever sent the little fucker, he's now dead. How do you want me to proceed?" She listened as Kane spoke for several minutes before he finally hung up. She flipped her own phone closed and turned to tell Malcolm what to expect. Her head swiveled right and left to nothing. He'd disappeared.

Reluctant to get too close to the body, she walked the long way around to the back of the house and knocked on the door there. He'd better be there.

"It's open."

Malcolm stood at the low bar against the back wall pouring a generous glass of what looked like whiskey.

"Want some?"

"Yes." She wasn't much of a drinker but the occasion seemed to call for it.

He splashed some liquid into a second tumbler and handed it over without a word. He took the seat across the room and they sat in silence drinking their alcohol and no doubt reliving the image of the mangled body outside.

"So what did he say?" His question brought her out of her thoughts and back into the here and now she wanted to avoid. The tension in the room that still carried the scent of their sex was so thick it was hard to think straight.

"Not to move the body and that someone would be flying in within the hour." He nodded. "Is leaving the body like it is going to cause any problems? We don't want to have to deal with the regular authorities as well."

"Ranger station is closed today but you never know who might wander in. I should probably do something to cover it up. I think I've got some tarps out in the garage that'll do the trick."

She set her drink on the table and stood to help him. "Cool, let's get it over with."

"No, I can do this myself," he snapped, his eyes blazing.

She held up her hands in surrender. "Fine, be all He-Man about it. I'd rather not look at the body again if I can help it."

She swiped at the glass bringing it up to her lips and gulping down the rest of it in one swallow. The liquid burned its way down her throat all the way to her belly and she didn't care. Whatever it took to ease the emotions Malcolm aroused in her whether it be anger or lust, it was going to drive her mad if she didn't get out soon.

CHAPTER
FIVE

Malcolm rifled through the garage, pushing things out of his way with a little more force than necessary. His emotions were out of control and he had no idea how to stop it.

Between the dead body at his doorstop and the rage over his mate's betrayal, his body burned from the inside out. For a brief moment in time, he'd believed an end to his miserable existence had arrived. No one completely understood the implications of an actual bond mate, but he'd had a chance to find out. But she was already mated so why the fuck did his body burn even worse for a woman that belonged to another?

Fuck. Just the thought of her with another man had his fingers tightening painfully on the roll of tarp in his hands. He needed to do something about this or whoever showed up to investigate wouldn't believe a word he said. Not with blood lust coursing through his veins. He probably looked ready to kill at any moment.

Malcolm stalked to the side door and headed to the front of the house, anxious to get this job done and out of the house. Until the cleaners arrived he'd put some distance between him and her luscious scent. For once in his life, he wanted to do the right thing and going back in the house to have drinks with the woman he ached for was not it.

Clearly he'd fucked up all those years ago, but what kind of woman cheated on her mate? Then she'd gone and reminded him of just who she was. A white furred shifter capable of becoming a wolf or a cougar. Not all hybrids had power like that. It made them sneaky as hell and hard to detect. Not to mention outcast. No wonder she snuck around all the damn time.

With her hybrid status, he knew she was normally confined to the neutral zone. But with her abilities she'd be a member of the inner clan. A group of polys who were called upon for dirty work or the kind of work no one else wanted. His father had told him about them, but over the years he'd begun to chalk them up as legend. Not once had Kane or Lucas mentioned them. Clearly he'd been gone too long if Kane was using them.

He needed to have a talk with his brothers. No! He wasn't an enforcer anymore so what the clan did had nothing more to do with him. The council had decided he wasn't worth saving after all. So why the hell would his brother send her here, for him?

Chey was right about one thing though. Her people were not thought of in a positive light by either cougar or wolf. They were caught in the middle and left alone because they were useful when they needed to be and quiet when they weren't. He had a hunch they'd downplayed their abilities though. Something about Chey seemed off and he suspected if either of the councils got wind of what they were missing out on, the enforcers would be hunting them down. And if one of them started killing people...

Before he even rounded the corner to the front of the house the nasty stench assaulted him. He sure hoped the cleaner Kane sent arrived soon; this wasn't a situation he wanted lingering at his front door. He'd been so angry when he'd left the house that when he'd found Chey leaned over the deceased she might as well have had blood smeared on her hands. He'd assumed the worst. Would his rejection have been enough to drive her over the ledge into a killing frenzy? It seemed unlikely. So who else had something to gain by killing Carl and leaving him on his doorstep?

Malcolm shook his head. None of this made any sense. Chey, Carl, Kane... It was all too planned. Malcolm stared down at all the jagged tears and gaping wounds that covered Carl. This was not a nice, clean kill. More like an outburst of provoked violence or the result of someone losing their mind. Or at least made to look like that. It seemed the more time passed the more suspicious he became.

Either way, the only suspects at this point would be he and Chey. They'd both been alone, in the vicinity, with motive and no alibi. In other words, they were fucked.

"Carl, why'd you have to go and get yourself killed? The least you could have done was find a way to leave us a clue." Talking to the dead seemed pointless but his frustration needed to go somewhere other than the woman sitting in his living room. Not even a cold, cruel murder stopped the yearning he felt for her, despite knowing the truth.

Malcolm blew out a hard breath. He only had to spend a little more time with her before the others arrived, invading his space and masking her scent with their own stink. He finished covering his once childhood friend who'd had his own secrets and hopped in his truck to move it so that anyone coming up the gravel road wouldn't see the tarp at his door and get curious.

Walking back toward the garage, Malcolm's nose flared at the slightest shift in the air. A strange scent carried on the wind, barely discernible even to him. He followed it trying to pick up a trail. Maybe he had just found the killer. If he didn't already have her.

The subtle odor led away from the house and into the woods. Malcolm contemplated whether or not it was a good idea to leave Chey alone and decided he couldn't pass up the only potential clue he'd found. She likely wouldn't run, but if she did, he would find her. His animal was certain of it. She still had some explaining to do. Malcolm quickly shed his clothes and attempted to shift to the cougar. If he was going to pursue through the woods he would have to do it as the animal; it would be easier to cover more ground.

Pain splintered in his skull, sending what felt like thousands of needles pushing through his skin. He stumbled to the forest floor on his hands and knees. Bones wrenched and contorted in an agony he couldn't bear. Screams pierced his ears under the onslaught of tearing flesh. Malcolm jerked as he fell to his side. Burning heat raged inside him, fast and out of control.

"Malcolm!" Through the rage and helplessness inside him he heard his mate calling for him. Fear tore through him the closer Chey got to him. His stomach pitched at the picture she would soon face. Him helpless to the torture of his own body. When had the situation progressed to this point? He'd shifted what, two, maybe three days before. The enraged beast inside him fought for total control, making logic impossible.

"Jesus fucking Christ, Malcolm." She dropped to her knees and moved to touch him.

"No!" He reared away from her. "Don't touch me."

"What the hell happened? Your body." Tears fell down her face while the burning pain raced through his blood. Somehow the scent of her fear broke through his consciousness and he wrestled the animal for control.

"What can I do? There has to be something." The trembling in her voice threatened to break him. He couldn't allow her suffering.

"Will be fine. Give me a minute," he pressed through gritted teeth.

"Oh Goddess."

His bones compressed and shifted again, this time to their normal state. The agony ripping through him recessed.

"I'll be fine in a few minutes. I just need to breathe." He tried to stretch an arm to only be greeted by more misery.

"What were you doing out here? Did someone do this to you?"

"No," he gasped. "Scent. Smelled something. Had to follow."

A frown crossed Chey's face and she tipped her nose into the air. "I can't smell beyond your suffering."

"Someone was here." He had to stop talking and focus on regaining control of his traitorous body.

A faint sound caught their attention and both he and Chey tilted their heads to peer through the canopy of trees. The sound grew louder until he finally recognized the thwap thwap of a helicopter moving in and doing so at a fast clip. Either they'd gotten here a lot faster than expected or he'd been out here far longer than he realized.

Fuck. The cleaners.

"Can't let them see me like this." Thank goddess for the thick sheltering pines of the forest. But he still had to recover quickly or be found out. "Can you stall them?"

"I'm not leaving you like this."

He grabbed her arm and winced at the torment the sudden move created. "You have to leave me. I need more time."

She stared down at him, tears falling down her cheeks. "Are you sure?"

"Yes. Now go."

She slowly stood and his eyes widened in shock. "Uhm, Chey honey. Where the fuck are your clothes?"

"I shifted when I heard your screams. I thought you were dying."

He'd thought so too. Although he hadn't realized all that screaming he'd heard had come from his own mouth. "Take my shirt. It's behind the tree."

"I don't need—"

He growled. "Take the damned shirt."

On a frustrated huff, she walked behind him and he heard the satisfying sound of cloth brushing her silken skin. The pain was slowly receding but not as quickly as the helicopter approached. She only had a few minutes to get back to the house.

"Hurry. Go now."

He sensed her hesitation but only for a second before she turned and ran. He heaved a sigh of relief and fell on his back. The ache and stiffness of his muscles hurt like hell but he couldn't lie here and wait for it to get better. Malcolm pushed to his feet despite the trembling of his arms and legs while balancing himself against the tree. Pure adrenalin fueled him now.

He reached for his jeans, and in warped and painful slow motion, he managed to get them on. A sheen of sweat covered his entire body from the effort of movement. Malcolm leaned against the tree and surveyed the area around him. The grassy area he'd stopped in disappeared in between rock croppings and dense trees, leaving nowhere for someone to make a trail. And with the dangerous terrain, it was unlikely the intruder had been human, although the damage to the body already told him that. If the killer had come through here there was no sign of him or her as it may be. Except for the faint scent of something unnatural he'd detected earlier. The evil in it could not be ignored.

Malcolm crouched and sniffed at the base of the tree, and his lip curled at the distinct stench of sweat and urine. Whoever he followed had rested here but it had been a while ago. He put his nose to the ground and searched for a direction from the rock and came up with nothing. Whoever it was had gone to a lot of trouble to hide their scent and knew how to do it well.

He stretched his muscles one last time and turned away from the tree. Like it or not, he couldn't wait any longer. He had to get to the ranger station. Judging the short distance he'd traveled in comparison to the sound of the helicopter landing, he'd only be a few minutes behind them.

Chey getting interrogated without him was not an option. He needed to assess who Kane had sent and what kind of clean up and investigation they had in mind. He pushed his body as hard as he could take and limped from the edge of the forest all while the savage beast inside him snarled in complaint. Malcolm contained him for now but if he left his mate with strangers for long, things would go south quickly.

Malcolm tried to remind himself that she belonged to another and wasn't his but his soul denied it. Watching the tears fall down her face when she'd cried over his injuries broke something inside him. They were about to have an even bigger problem besides the investigation. Despite the evidence of her mating, he wanted her. Goddess help him, he couldn't let her go.

He took a shortcut through the back of the property thanks to his knowledge of the terrain. He'd hit this town in a desperate need to get away from his old life and somehow managed to stay. When Jeff the ranger asked him to watch over the park for him, he never dreamed it would be for months. He should have been long gone by now. Maybe if Chey hadn't found him so effortlessly, Carl would still be alive.

He burst through the trees into the clearing on the side of the house to find the helicopter had indeed already landed in the open field about three hundred yards from where he stood. He circled behind the house to go through the garage. He wanted to catch a glimpse of his visitors before they saw him.

Malcolm rounded the corner of the house at the same time Chey stepped out of the side door making a crash inevitable. Her shoulder and arm dug into his chest and her leg tangled around his, pitching her forward toward the dirt. With restored reflexes, Malcolm automatically reached for her and caught her around the waist before she planted herself on the ground face first.

That brief physical contact fired his blood and made his groin tighten with renewed desire for the woman in his arms. The one his primitive side still called mate. Her gaze settled on his face, and for a few brief seconds he recognized the same lustful reaction in the blazing blue eyes staring back at him. Her lips parted, and a warm sweet breath of air feathered across his face to further entice him, begging him to take a taste.

"Are you okay?" she whispered.

"If by okay you mean hard as a rock and ready to fuck, then yeah, I'm fine."

Chey's brow arched. "Yeah I'd say you're back to your old self then." She shoved at his chest. "You can put me down now."

Malcolm bit back a laugh. She spoke words of piss and vinegar but the husky tone of her voice gave her away. It took grinding his teeth together for all he was worth to keep from kissing her senseless.

"You should be more careful where you're going. There's still a killer on the loose, right?" He watched the fury bloom across her face at his insinuation.

"Right." Her response dripped in sarcasm as she uttered it. Good. She needed to know that she was not off the hook as far as he was concerned. Her kindness in the woods had only softened his heart momentarily until the images of her with another man bled through his brain again.

"The chopper landed."

"So I heard."

"Might as well go and greet whoever Kane sent. Have you already talked to them? We probably should have discussed this before they got here. You know, what we wanted to say."

"I'm not the one that left the house twice."

"And I'm not the one who belongs to another man." Yeah, it was nasty, but he couldn't help himself. This whole situation was a cluster fuck and a half.

She wrenched from his grip and shoved his shoulder against the house. Turning, she walked away in the direction of the helicopter, leaving him to watch her sashay her way across the yard. Malcolm shook his head. For someone who still had a lot of explaining to do she had quite an attitude. Haughty wench. Good thing he had other problems to distract him. The frustration of not being able to claim her continued to grow with every passing minute he spent touching her. The animal inside had risen with no intention of backing down despite all the flimsy protests she fired his way. The illogical need to take her began to consume him. Evidenced by his hardened cock pressed painfully against binding denim simply from catching her fall. The cat didn't give a damn whether she was willing or not.

Despite the danger lurking nearby, with her scent wrapped around him it took focus born of brutal intensity to keep from hauling her to the ground. If a council helicopter had not just landed, he might not have been able to resist the urge she brought out in him. The one that needed her tied to his bed, submitting to him...

He wanted to say something, make her stop walking away even for a second so he blurted out the first thing he could think of.

"I picked up a scent." She froze midstep without looking back. "That's what I was doing in the woods. Someone tried to cover it but they underestimated my tracking ability. If I'd been able to shift I might have found more. Whoever we are dealing with is very smart about what they're doing. We need to be careful."

She turned back to face him, her expression unreadable. "And why weren't you able to shift?"

Good going, bright one. Why don't you just tell her you suck while you're at it? "That's a story for another time, darling. Right now we have company. Better get your story straight."

She snarled in his direction before turning and walking away, leaving him as frustrated as before. Her cool as ice demeanor every time he threw a barb her way gave nothing away. But if she didn't do this, who did? What possible motivation could they have? His head throbbed with the endless barrage of questions he came up with, not to mention the onslaught they were about to receive.

He spied two people walking their way from the clearing. He recognized the man right away as Ben Hawling. Council assistant and hard ass extraordinaire. The woman he didn't know at all. Short, cropped blond hair and blindingly pale skin, she stood to Ben's shoulder if she was lucky. With a few quick strides, he caught up to Chey and went with her to face them. Whether she knew it or not they needed to provide a united front. Unless something came up pretty quick they would be the only suspects and their asses would be on the line.

Ben's grim face didn't smile or frown when he stopped in front of them. No, he knew how to control his emotions. "Malcolm." He nodded to the man as he turned to Chey and held out his hand. "I'm Ben Hawling, the Council representative that Kane Gunn sent to assess the situation."

"Is that the politically correct way to say you're here to nail someone's ass for a murder?" Bitter ice-cold eyes snapped over to him, assessing the situation.

"You know better than anyone how this works. There are customs and laws to be upheld, even for you."

Malcolm growled at Ben in warning, he wasn't about to put up with the man coming in here and pissing all over him just to prove a point. The petite woman stepped forward, angling herself between the two men.

"Hi, I'm Charlie." She held out her hand and Malcolm reluctantly took it while stealing a glance at Chey who stood stoically next to him, keeping her facial features as calm as possible. A subtle sense of power moved through him when he touched the woman, taking him aback. "I'm here to represent Chey in this investigation."

"You're one of..." He let his words trail off because he couldn't think of any way to say it without it being taken as an insult of some sort.

"If by that you mean a hybrid, then yes. Not all of us are ashamed of the word." She smiled at him with her statement but it was the kind of look that wasn't really a smile but a "you better not fuck with me" expression.

"Actually no, I was referring to the other."

"The other?" Now all of them were staring at him like he'd grown a third head. As if they had no clue what he was talking about.

"Yeah, when you shook my hand I felt a whisper of it."

"Malcolm," Ben interrupted. "You've been away from the clan for a while and things have changed. We have a treaty now with the polys so don't go pissing all over it and giving me extra work to do."

Charlie turned to Chey then, giving her a hard and assessing look. "I don't think Mr. Gunn meant any harm. Maybe we should get a move on and take a look at that body. We're burning daylight and we've got a clean up to take care of."

"Uh huh." Malcolm let the questions burning at the tip of his tongue die and turned back to the house. He didn't give a crap about treaties and the politics that went along with them. His primary concern was getting both he and Chey out of this mess with their lives. Or at least hers. With the episode back in the trees it would appear his clock would soon run out. Maybe he would find this mate of hers and ensure she'd be well taken care of. The cat howled inside his head in protest. *Too bad, so sad buddy. If this is the end of the road her life is more important.*

He led them around front where he'd left the body covered and blocked by his vehicle. Except... He halted in his tracks, Chey crashing into his back.

There was no body.

The bright blue tarp flapped in the wind against the side of his truck while the gravel and dirt in front of his house lay perfectly still and pristine.

"What the hell?" Both he and Chey ran forward, skidding to a stop right where the gruesome body had lain a scant few hours ago.

"What's wrong? What's going on here?"

Malcolm turned and looked at the hard demand in Ben's face before he glanced at Chey. "This is where we found the body this morning. Right here where we're standing." Tension arced through him as Chey's emotions radiated off of her. Distrust, anger, frustration all underlined by the scent of her arousal.

"So, where did you move it to and why?" Ben's condescending tone made the hair on his neck stand on end. Malcolm's peeled his lips back and bared his teeth. Anger whipped through him. He wasn't about to take shit from this man or field stupid questions. He tightened his hands, his claws extended and ready to attack at a moment's notice.

"Malcolm." A soft touch landed on his arm and he whirled around coming face to face with Chey, her eyes soft and reassuring. "It's okay; they're just here to do their job."

He shook off her arm. "Stop already with the woo woo stuff. They aren't here to help," he hissed. "They're going to arrest one of us for this and you damn well know it."

"Enough." Charlie stepped forward and addressed Malcolm. "If you don't want us to jump to any conclusions here, then you damn well better give us the same benefit of the doubt. We're here to help."

Malcolm eyed her cautiously while he struggled to compose himself by pushing the animal back. "I didn't move the body. I covered it and left it right here."

Ben pulled gloves from his pocket and pulled them onto his hands. "Okay, then I imagine Chey here can corroborate that. You left the body here and then the two of you did what?" He pulled the tarp loose from where it had attached underneath the corner of the bumper and scanned it for trace evidence. He exchanged a knowing look with Charlie before he proceeded to visually inspect the area underneath the truck. Eventually he realized that no one had answered him and he turned to peer over his shoulder at them. "Well?"

"I left Chey in the house while I took care of this and then I went for a walk in the woods until I heard the helicopter approaching."

Ben groaned and stood back up to his full height. "Tell me you're kidding. You're pissed that we're here and now you're just being sarcastic, right?"

Malcolm stared at him, willing himself not to roll his eyes at the man staring him down with disbelief shining in his eyes.

"Jesus fucking Christ. What were you thinking? Someone should have been standing guard over this body until we got here. You of all people know procedure." He shook his head and threw the tarp into the bed of Malcolm's pickup.

"Maybe I forgot. Seeing how I've been gone from the clan for so long." Malcolm mimicked Ben's words from earlier with an extra heavy dose of sarcasm.

Ben glared him.

"If the two of you are done measuring your dicks now, I think we should conduct a thorough perimeter search and if that doesn't produce anything then we'll move straight into separate interviews." Charlie didn't hesitate or wait for any response. She simply walked away to begin her search, leaving them all to stare after her.

Yeah, this was definitely a colossally fucked up mess.

CHAPTER
SIX

C haos. The pawns in his game were pissed off and frustrated over the disappearance of the body. Perfect.

He watched them from the trees at a safe distance away and downwind so no scent would be detected. If panic set in the situation would go from bad to worse in the blink of an eye. They'd be too busy covering their asses to bother with clan business, leaving Kane on his own. The situation with Malcolm was getting out of control. As soon as he'd gotten wind that the half-breed bitch had hooked up with Kane in an attempt to return his brother to the clan, he'd had to make a move. Divide and conquer or simply sit back and watch them implode.

The last thing he needed right now was for them to get a clue. Every time he got close to shutting them all out of the clan they'd managed to pull some luck out of their ass and thwart his plans. Now he just wanted them gone. Every time he delegated any responsibilities to someone else things went to hell, so this time he'd come himself to dispatch Carl. He'd been so angry when he'd arrived in this neck of the woods. There'd been only one direction to send his rage. He pictured the moment clearly. The fear on the shifter's face had been incredible.

His heart beat wildly every time he remembered. Killing had been easier than he thought. John had been his first and now this... The animal inside roared with pleasure. He already wanted another hunt. The taste of blood on his tongue and the pungent smell of prey lured him to the surface.

For the man, the fun part was dumping him on Malcolm's doorstep and watching everyone come apart at the seams. He and his little freak ought to have fun explaining that one. There were plenty of human witnesses that could offer up information about Malcolm's confrontation with Carl early that morning.

Luckily, he'd not been far when the call from Carl had come through. He'd fucked up and gotten spotted by

Malcolm. That dirty bastard didn't deserve the blood running through his veins. All of it should have been his. As the first-born male in his family, he'd been expected to carry the gene and serve his family. Instead he'd suffered through his childhood in his younger-by-ten minutes brother's shadow as the inferior twin.

He didn't care what it took to make things right or who he had to kill to do it. Those boys would not continue their inferior bloodline if it was the last thing he did. All the hard work and effort he'd put into getting rid of them without suspicion on himself was about to pay off. And once the clan was without its guardian he could make his move to take over the council. He sat heavily on a rock and blew out a hard breath. This moment had been coming for so long. As the only true blood heir, he'd take what rightfully belonged to him and make sure his brother's dirty mongrels were left with nothing.

Soon it would be time for it all to end. The years of patiently planning were wearing thin. If Malcolm or Kane interfered again, then he'd just gut them and be done with it. A vibration in his pocket signaled an incoming call. He pulled the small device from his pants and examined the screen.

His sniveling, no good daughter was looking for him. That was another string that needed cutting. He pressed the button to decline the call and allowed a slow smile to curl his lips. *Oh yes, darling daughter, your usefulness has expired.*

CHAPTER
SEVEN

"How long were the two of you apart this morning before you found the body?" Charlie and Ben had been grilling her for what seemed like hours and many of the same questions had been asked over and over until Chey thought her head would explode. How many different ways could she answer the same questions?

"As I've told you countless times already I'm not sure. It didn't seem like very long but I wasn't watching the clock you know, I had other things on my mind."

"What other things, Chey?" Charlie just wouldn't let it go. She'd suspected every answer Chey'd given had more to it, that she was holding back.

And she was. She didn't want these two, of all people, to know what had been going on between her and Malcolm while Carl had been murdered. It would be mortifying to go down that road, especially with Charlie, who knew how dangerous she had become this past year.

"So you're saying at the time of the alleged murder you were inside the house mere feet away and heard nothing. That with your heightened sense of sound and smell you had no clue what was going on outside?"

Chey grabbed the small cup of water Charlie had offered and downed it in one fast gulp. Not that it was going to help her stall for much time. "That's right." And that's all they were going to get.

Ben slammed his hands down on the table. "Bullshit!"

Charlie grabbed Ben's arm and Chey swore she heard growling outside the room. They'd sequestered Malcolm at the opposite end of the house in his supposedly sound proofed media room. He shouldn't be able to hear a word of this interrogation.

Charlie leaned forward and whispered something in his ear. Chey could not pick up more than a brief sound of air. This woman was damned good. But where had she come from? It wasn't like there were thousands of her kinds roaming the woods. The clans were so rigid with their rules on interspecies breeding, that it was a rare breed who dared to defy them.

In fact, they'd only been given a small area in the neutral zone with everyone either working at the saloon or doing her kind of work.

"Look, Ms. Ross, we aren't here expressly to harass you. Only get to the bottom of what happened. Put yourself in our shoes and tell me what you'd do if you'd been sent into this situation to find a dead body missing and two people obviously withholding information. I dare say you'd be running out of patience as well."

"I'd say if there is no body then the whole thing must have been a figment of my imagination and you should let me go."

Ben snorted.

"Not likely, Chey. Now tell us what is going on between you and Malcolm Gunn. One minute he seems to want to kill you and the next kill one of us for getting too close to you. If we didn't know better we'd think..."

Charlie's eyes widened and Chey saw the truth in them. "But that's impossible."

"What's impossible? What the hell did I miss?" Ben glanced between the two women and Chey allowed her eyes to squeeze closed. Memories of John assaulted her out of nowhere, catching her off guard. He'd be so pissed at her for accepting this job. He'd suspected what Malcolm was to her five years ago and no matter how much she denied it, he never quite believed her.

"Malcolm thinks Chey is his mate."

The statement hit the room like a deafening bomb, leveling Chey where she sat. Having Charlie say the words out loud was like being stabbed in the gut with a dull knife. This was not at all how this was supposed to go.

"Is this true?" Charlie asked.

Chey didn't answer. Her brain refused the question.

"Fuck, this complicates the hell out of things. Does he know about John?"

Chey's eyes popped open and she stared daggers into Charlie. "How the hell do you know about John?"

Charlie rolled her eyes. "C'mon Cheyenne. You're smarter than that. Do you think I'd come in here not knowing every detail of your life? How else do you expect me to represent you if I don't know you?"

"You don't fucking know me. None of you do." Anger whipped through her as she lashed out. How dare they drag her past into this? "None of this has anything to do with John so leave him out of this."

"Who the hell is John?" Poor Ben sounded completely confused.

"Her dead mate."

Chey's stomach revolted and the crackers she'd managed to eat earlier threatened to return. She pressed her hand over her stomach and bent at the waist and vomited on the floor.

"Ben, give us a few minutes okay?"

Chey heard the scraping of Ben's chair and the steps he took toward the door. Her stomach heaved the entire time even after the door closed behind the man.

"Do you need some more water?" Charlie's voice had lowered and softened. Waves of sympathy washed over Chey.

"I need nothing," she croaked.

"You need some help in this situation and damned fast that's what you need, Chey. You are minutes away from being arrested and hauled into cougar territory with your new lover. This is not going to go over well."

"Without a body you can't accuse Malcolm or I of anything. Don't try to play me for a fool here."

Hopelessness tore through her despite the bravado she gave this woman. She'd already lost everything that meant anything she honestly didn't care what they wanted to do.

"Don't be so sure about that, Ms. Ross. We already have on record from the both of you that a body existed, and, unless the man in question comes walking through that door anytime soon, someone will go down for this murder."

Chey's stomach heaved again despite being bone dry at this point. It was happening all over again. First John and now this.

"You've killed before. It gave you a taste of bloodlust didn't it? Is that what happened here?" Charlie had come around the table and crouched beside her. She taunted Chey with her past. "Killing John wasn't enough. You had to have another. So tell me, crippled half-breed. Who's next?"

Wood splintered and flew around her. Chey ducked and swiveled prepared to fight whoever or whatever had come crashing in the room. Before she even got a glimpse, hard, restraining fingers clamped around her arm and hauled her to her feet.

"Malcolm, whaat theee hellll?" Her words slurred. Something was seriously wrong.

"What's going on? What did you do to her?"

Malcolm shook her while glaring at Charlie with his questions.

"Control yourself, cougar. It's nothing out of the ordinary. She's only been given a mild sedative that lowers her inhibitions. She hasn't been exactly forthcoming."

"So you drugged her."

Ben rushed through the door and blocked Malcolm from moving any closer to Charlie. "Sorry. I tried to stop him but he's wilier than he looks."

"Fuck you, Ben. You were a part of this?"

"Neither one of you is cooperating all that well. One of you is lying and from the looks of it, the other is helping."

Malcolm brushed the hair from her face and cradled her to his chest. "You son of a bitch. When this is over, I'll be coming for you."

"Don't threaten me, Malcolm. I have full council approval to use whatever methods are available to me to get to the facts."

"You want facts?" He lifted Chey into his arms. "We didn't do shit. While Carl was getting himself killed, I was alone with Chey discovering that she wasn't who I thought she was."

Chey glanced upward, too weak to move but more than alert enough to hear the pain behind Malcolm's words.

"What the hell is that supposed to mean? If you have some kind of evidence that proves your innocence, now is the time to produce it."

"It has nothing to do with the murder."

Ben stepped close—too close. "I think you should let me be the judge of that."

Malcolm growled, the vibrations running through his chest and into her body tucked at his side. "Slowly step back before I do something we will both regret."

The venom in Malcolm's voice dripped with malice. If Ben had half a brain at this point, he'd better move.

"What's wrong, Malcolm? Am I making you uncomfortable? What's the big deal?"

Damn it. Now Ben was just baiting him. "Malcolm, don't listen to him." In Chey's head, the words she spoke came out fine but the way he and Ben were eyeing her made it pretty clear she'd spoken gibberish.

Ben turned back to Charlie. "How much did you give her?"

"Less than the dose you recommended. I assumed you gave me what you thought a typical cougar would need but her metabolism is a little different."

"Enough. We're done talking to you." Malcolm made to move around Ben and the other man adjusted his position to further block them from leaving.

"I don't think so. Just because you're feeling a little protective over your new toy doesn't exempt you from the law."

"How dare you speak about my mate like that!"

Charlie and she gasped at the same time. Ben only smiled. "Finally we might be getting somewhere. The truth isn't nearly as bitter as you think it is."

"I wouldn't count on that." Chey spoke the words as slowly as possible, being careful to enunciate every syllable correctly. "He's not my mate."

She caught the wince on Malcolm's face a moment before he cleared it. Chey did her best to harden her heart toward it. The last thing she could afford now was to put another man in danger. Even an arrogant ass, who probably deserved it, like him.

"She's right. When you cling to a lie long enough you begin to believe it. In this case it's definitely not true. She is already mated."

"That's hardly a consideration anymore."

Chey glared at Ben and struggled in Malcolm's arms. "Put me down."

"No." The cool grimace he aimed in her direction dared her to defy him. "Like I said. We're done here. If and when you find a shred of evidence that implicates either one of us, you can give me a call. For now, I'd say your actions have rendered you lucky to still be alive."

The savage look on Malcolm's face gave her pause. No matter how insolent or stubborn he behaved it would behoove her to remember who and what he was. They both might share some cougar blood but the results were drastically different. The DNA of a black cougar produced an animal far more lethal than the rest of the clan. Not to mention the man. Even now with her dulled responses and dangerous situation, the hard corded body pressed to hers awakened senses she'd tried to force dormant. She wanted him. Fiercely.

If she wasn't very, very careful, she'd become his prey before she even realized what had happened.

"Did she bother to tell you the circumstances surrounding her mate's death?"

Chey felt every muscle in Malcolm's body freeze. She racked her brain for something—anything to say that would stop the train that had just been derailed. Fucking cougars.

Chey met Malcolm's gaze and winced at the hard edge of anger and suspicion in his eyes. For a few lingering seconds it was as if time stood still and they were the only two people in the room. She knew he was giving her a chance to say something but she couldn't. If Ben was going to paint her as a murderess, might as well let Malcolm hear it now. Once he did then maybe the mate business between them would finally be settled. No man wanted a woman as cold as she'd been.

When she firmly clamped her mouth shut, awareness dawned in Malcolm's eyes and he turned back to Ben.

"Excuse me?" Ice dripped from those two words, as if the room had gone dark and frigid.

For the second time in one short year, Chey was terrified. Obviously the cloud around John's death had not been contained to neutral ground. Ben was about to reveal her darkest moments to the one man she'd never stopped loving. Tears burned in her eyes but refused to be shed. Every nightmare she'd endured would all be for nothing the moment he learned the truth. Images of that blood soaked night ripped through her mind, tearing once again at the frayed edges of her sanity. If she'd been the wife John deserved none of this would have ever happened.

The adrenalin coursing through her managed to break through some of the drugged stupor. She swung her arms and struggled against Malcom's strength. Freedom. She had to have it now. "Let me go," she whispered.

"Never." His muted response shivered along her skin. "Tell me."

She didn't know whom he'd directed his demand to, but it was Ben who opened his mouth and spoke.

"It was her personal knife that we found buried in her mate's chest. I doubt there's a soul in any clan that doesn't believe she didn't do it. Unfortunately our council doesn't have jurisdiction over non-clan members and her family refused to execute her based on what they termed circumstantial evidence. But..."

Oh God, where was he going with this? The sound of his voice had gone from smug to almost amused. Was he laughing at her situation?

"If she's your mate now I believe that changes the rules."

"Now hold on Ben. This isn't about ancient history. We were sent here to clean up a recent murder, not rehash the past."

Finally someone stood up for her. Even if Charlie rubbed her wrong and Chey wanted to slit her throat for drugging her.

"Your mate is dead?" For a second, Malcolm's hold loosened and she slid to her knees with his hands grasping her arms.

A scream of fresh grief tore through her head at the simple question. She had no idea how to handle this. She sucked in gulps of air trying to breathe. Her fault. She did this. She had to pay for it. No matter how many times she begged for a second chance nothing ever changed. She woke up alone and broken day after day, guilt slowly eating her away.

"Chey! Answer me." His fingers tightened on her arm as he gave her a firm shake.

"I warned Kane not to send me here. This wasn't supposed to happen." She clawed at his arms, desperate to pry him loose.

"Tell me damn it." He dipped his head to her ear. "I'm not letting you out of here until you answer me. Is. Your. Mate. Dead?"

Chey stared into Malcolm's face. She hated him as much as she loved him. John had known and didn't care. He'd tried to give her everything and in the end she'd failed. Tears clouded her vision making it impossible for her to focus on Malcolm. Instead she breathed deeply of his scent. So much anger surrounded him and pain. Oh God. Her stomach heaved.

"Yes," she cried, sure in the knowledge that he would never forgive her. What he'd done all those years ago paled in comparison. Mate or no mate, some things could never be forgiven. Her stomach wrenched painfully and she grabbed her waist mere seconds before throwing up all over his feet.

CHAPTER
EIGHT

For the first time in too many years, Malcolm felt a sliver of hope. He had no idea what the hell was going on here or why they thought she'd killed her mate, but through the wild terror he scented from her he still felt hope.

Although something was seriously wrong here. What he sensed from Chey had nothing to do with fear and everything to do with guilt and pain. He had to get to the whole truth. First things first. He lifted her shivering frame into his arms and walked from the room. He vaguely heard voices in the background ordering him to stop, all of which he ignored. His mate needed him and for once in his life he wasn't going to disappoint her.

He carried her down the hall and into his bedroom. With his foot he kicked the door shut behind him, confident that no one would dare follow him. The anger had boiled to the surface and one glance at the female had told him all he needed to know. Her fear at the sight of him meant one thing. His eyes glowed molten gold of the cougar, warning her. His skin itched and his bones ached. With the strength born of years of hard earned discipline he tightened the leash on the animal inside him and focused on Chey instead.

With slow, precise movements he entered the bathroom and gingerly stood her on her feet. "You okay to stand for a second?"

She nodded, the pain in her eyes tearing through his heart. Malcolm steadied her before reaching for the glass-enclosed shower. "I'm going to get you cleaned up and give you some time to pull it together. Then we're going to talk."

The glazed expression in her gaze didn't change.

Automatically, he reached for the shower controls and turned the water and heat to full blast. He returned to her side and began to strip away her clothes. He curled his fingers around the bottom of her shirt and lifted it over her head and tossed it toward the laundry basket. His throat closed at the sight of her lush breasts only barely covered by a few scraps of silk and lace. As much as he ached to touch her—to get inside her, the haunted look in her eyes stopped him. After a deep and not so calming breath, he unzipped her pants and slid them from her legs.

The minute he'd learned her mated status wasn't exactly as she'd presented, his brain had gone into overdrive. The cat clawed at his mind to take what belonged to him but the man hesitated. There was too much he didn't know or understand yet.

"You're dirty too," she whispered.

"I know. But don't worry about me." He turned her away from him and eased her in the direction of the shower stall. Before he opened the door, he divested her of her bra. Next, he peeled the panties from her legs and she stepped out of them. Malcolm ground his teeth together as he fought to stay in control. If he touched her any more there were no guarantees he could stop himself from taking her.

His eyes narrowed on the delectable curves of her ass while the hunger ate him from the inside out. The lust raging through his body threatened his sanity as well as the logic he sought. She suddenly turned to him and stared into his eyes.

"Please don't leave me." Chey pulled her bottom lip between her teeth. "Not yet."

Malcolm growled a response deep in his throat. Words deserted him. He lifted her into the shower and stepped in behind her fully clothed. Hot water splashed across her skin and made it glisten. She shifted in his embrace, attempting to turn around. His arms tightened, immobilizing her.

"Don't. I only have so much control."

Chey stilled. He inhaled deeply, imprinting her scent. His body went impossibly harder and he bit back a groan. He'd never get enough of her to satisfy the man or the animal. Malcolm reached for the soap and lathered his hands. He'd come this far, might as well go for broke. At the first touch of his hands to her bare back, Chey sucked in a sharp breath. He knew exactly how she felt. Dear God her skin felt like heaven under his touch.

She dipped her head under the spray and soaked her hair. That simple move revealed the mark he needed to avoid. The birthmark on her neck that marked her as a bond mate. The small scar in the middle of it burned in his gut. The mere thought of another man's mouth on his mark threatened his sanity. His hands clenched into tight fists while he beat back the urge to take.

Bite her.

The animal inside taunted him.

Claim her now.

Malcolm clamped his jaw together tight. No. The last thing in the world he should do right now was tie her to him forever. If he died, and that possibility was growing stronger with each passing day, she would die as well.

The thought struck him like a dagger to the heart. He whipped Chey around. "You were bitten. Your mark claimed. If your mate is really dead, why are you still alive?"

She shrugged. The look in her eyes so pain-filled it nearly cut him to his knees. "I don't think it works with just anyone," she whispered, barely to be heard over the roar in his ears.

Malcolm mulled her response in his mind. If that were true then whomever she'd tried to mate with before had failed. They may have had feelings for each other but the mate bond had not been achieved. He looked into her large beautiful eyes, searching for something —anything to give him more hope. The instinctive need to take her ripped through his senses even harder. He wanted to be the one. The only one. His canines ached. It seemed the more he fought it the harder the cougar struggled.

He grabbed a handful of her hair and tipped her head back until the water sluiced over her once again. This position exposed her neck to his gaze, a fact she didn't fight against. Yet, instead of taking what he was desperate for, the memory of her pain grabbed him by the balls. As much as he needed to be buried inside her wet heat, fucking until they both collapsed, he hesitated.

"It's not safe for you to be with me," he admitted.

She pressed her fingertips to the side of his face, the heat nearly burning him through. "I'm willing to take my chances."

Malcolm groaned and leaned forward, his teeth grazing the column of her neck. "You smell so fucking good."

She threaded her fingers through his hair, holding him tight. "Take what you need."

Oh fuck. He was so screwed. He'd fight it. She'd been drugged, simple as that. If she were in her right mind she wouldn't even be allowing him near her. So he'd take...a little.

Malcolm fought the arousal until it simmered underneath the surface instead of boiling out of control. He brushed his cheek across hers, simply reveling in the heat of her touch. "If and when we ever go any further again, it will not be when you're high on some drug or your judgment impaired in any other manner. If there is a next time, it will be because it's what you want more than your next breath." If she didn't ache for it like he did it would kill him.

"Malcolm," she purred, her hands tightening on his head.

His nostrils flared at the sudden and overwhelming scent of her desire filling the shower stall. His name on her sweet lips unraveled a little more of his control.

"No." He whispered into her ear, his lips barely touching her. "Not like this." Reluctantly, he pulled free of her embrace and did his level best not to look down. He reached for the shampoo and filled his palm with the strong scent of lavender. Anything to take his mind off Chey's intoxicating musk. "Turn around." The command came out far harsher than he'd intended.

Without another word she did as he asked, and with no ability to stop himself, he glanced down at the sweet heart shaped ass he coveted. God help him, he needed divine intervention to stop himself from bending her over in front of him and sinking balls deep no matter what he thought was best for them both. His body throbbed like a son of a bitch and the memories of their sex earlier that day filled his head like a movie set on automatic replay to torture him.

He jerked his fingers into her hair and began lathering the strands with shampoo. Why he insisted on making this more difficult for them both evaded him. But for whatever reason he could not take his hands off of her. He'd been at the opposite side of the house pacing when he'd sensed her acute distress. The scent of it had rammed him and sent him staggering for a few seconds before he regained a modicum of equilibrium.

He'd rushed toward the room they were using to interrogate her and come face to face with Ben. He'd growled for the other man to get out of his way to no avail. Since getting into a fight with another cougar would take away precious time, he'd ran through the house, using his knowledge of the layout to his advantage and beating Ben to the room by a mere few seconds.

Fuck. Even now the image of his mate on the floor grasping for control made him see blood red. In that moment, he'd wanted to pull the woman responsible limb from limb and then some. He'd had to fight the blood lust like never before in his life. If Chey hadn't needed him so much in that moment, he'd have found himself facing a different sort of murder charge. One that would have left him without a leg to stand on in their current situation.

Her knife.

The remembered words sliced through him. There were always two sides to a story and it sickened him that the council assholes would use this tactic to drive a wedge between them. They were perfectly capable of doing that themselves, thank you very much. These tactics were getting old and something needed to be done. Malcolm sighed. Not that he should care. They'd turned their backs on him long ago.

"Ouch."

Malcolm stared down at his fingers in her hair and relaxed his hold. "Sorry."

He finished washing her hair and bent her forward to rinse the suds from the lush mane. He swallowed hard. He'd been crazy to get this close to her like this. His erection throbbed against his now soaking wet and increasingly tight pants.

"You didn't have to do this," she whispered.

"Why did you lie to me?" Malcolm blurted without thinking. His need to know overrode his intentions to wait for this conversation.

She froze, her body going rigid under his touch. He sensed her reluctance to get into this with him.

"I didn't lie."

"Semantics, Chey. Don't even go there." His hold on control weakened to the point his blood raged through his veins. As much as he hated to shatter their time together, he couldn't stop himself.

She inhaled slowly. Likely buying time to decide what to tell him. At that moment he dared her to push back at him. With his desire for her ruling his thoughts and emotions, it wouldn't take much to shatter the thin thread of control holding him together.

"I don't want to have this conversation naked in the shower."

He ached to see her eyes. To watch the emotions moving through her like they did him. But she was right. They were on extremely dangerous ground. Malcolm clenched his teeth and forced the animal back. His fingers ached and he expected any moment for his claws to break free.

"I'll concede for now. But you need to understand that we will be discussing it and my patience is running thin." She wasn't going to run or hide from him again. He lowered his head, placing his mouth at the edge of her ear. "I can only hold the cougar back for so long, darling."

A hard shudder raced over her. Satisfied that he'd gotten her attention, he turned off the water and pulled her from the stall. His pants squished and tightened around him as he moved. Neither of which did a damn thing to help the fact he was rock hard and ready. He grabbed one of the bath towels and began drying her skin. He took care to be gentle and not rough her up anymore than she already had been. As the water dried, the natural scent of her musk rose from the opened pores of her skin.

Not inhaling wasn't an option. He couldn't get enough of her. His balls drew tight against his skin and the blood raced through his veins until it pooled in his heavy shaft. Never in his entire life had a woman made him ache like this. Despite, or maybe because of, her failed mating, his instincts told him it would not be the case between them. If he bit her like he ached to the results would be final and permanent. And it took every ounce of discipline he possessed not to rob her of the choice.

She was his woman.

He quickly wrapped a thick robe around her nude form before the claws of need shredded him any further. Once covered, he spun her to face him. "You can't hide from this. I won't allow it."

"I'm so tired, Malcolm. For a year I've wanted nothing but peace. It's never coming is it?"

That familiar pain swam in her eyes. This time it offended him. He wanted to snarl and demand, take and consume. "Probably not." This time he didn't bother to hide the resentment he felt. Their situation had turned beyond fucked up and she'd learn to deal. He cupped her chin and forced her gaze to meet his. "We are in this together though. Bad or good, you're stuck with me. I won't allow any other choice."

"Even if it means your death?"

Her question made no sense but his answer wouldn't change. "I'm not that easy to kill, sweetheart, so don't go getting any crazy ideas. And don't do anything to push me to make a decision we'll both regret."

Before he lost complete control and did something crazy, he dropped his hand and turned away. "Unless you are looking for me to lay you out on the bathroom floor and fuck you until neither of us can move, I suggest you give me a few minutes to get cleaned up."

She blinked, the surprise clearly etched on her face. A second later he could have sworn a challenge flared in her gaze before quickly being replaced with a carefully crafted blankness. "Don't challenge me, Malcolm. You won't like the results." She whirled around and stalked from the room. Clearly the shower had helped clear her head. He laughed. Her spit and fire had returned. Good. Now they could get down to business.

He peeled the heavy fabric from his legs and tossed them in the sink. He took in his ragged appearance in the mirror above it and grimaced. Slowly, he grasped the aching flesh between his legs and squeezed to the point of pain. There was so much he needed from Cheyenne and it went so far beyond a simple fuck. Was she even aware of his darker desires? The ones where it meant her tied to a wall so he could have his way with her?

He pulled hard on his dick, hoping the mixture of pain and pleasure would ease the intense pressure battling him at every turn. He imagined Chey on her knees in front of him, her mouth opening to take him inside.

He groaned at the agony that image created. His body ached. He pumped his hand several times, moaning at the agony and ecstasy of the moment. But Chey wasn't with him. She'd fled the bathroom and left him to his own business. Malcolm groaned and released his erection. He would not get what he needed like this. The only solution for him was ten feet on the other side of the door—waiting.

He moved to the shower and turned the water to frigid. If a cold shower couldn't relieve his own personal version of hell then God help Chey. Kane or fate had sent her here and he was spiraling out of control. Like it or not, what happened next was up to nature.

CHAPTER
NINE

They gripped the edge of the desk, willing the hunger devouring her to ease. Whatever drug that bitch had fed her still hovered at the edges of her brain. But she'd regained enough clarity to know how close she and Malcolm dangled on the edge of serious trouble. Every touch of his fingers on her skin had burned through the effects of the drug until the pressure between her legs had grown unbearable. One word from him and she would have gladly bent over and begged to be taken.

He'd entered the room moments ago but she was afraid to turn around and face him. He'd smell the arousal, she definitely couldn't hide that. One glance at him now and she'd be done. Cooked. Toast. Screwed.

Her nipples ached for the sweet heat of his mouth as he nipped and nibbled his way between them both. The skin from her hips to the aching bud of her mound felt on fire from simply imagining his touch there too.

"Jesus, Chey. Are you trying to kill me?"

"Don't go there. I know what your senses are picking up but let's simply chalk it up to an anomaly and let it go."

The air in the room shifted, the only indication Malcolm had moved until he hovered so close behind her his heat brushed over her in waves. "You're my mate. You don't have to suffer like this."

"I'm not your mate, I belong to..."

He pressed into her before she finished her sentence. His large body straddled her legs with the hard ridge of his erection pressing into her ass. The fact they both wore clothes seemed to mean little.

She gasped. Whether in protest or in pleasure she wasn't sure. This was certainly trouble with a capital T. "Stop," she pleaded.

"If you say you belong to another one more time I won't be held responsible for what happens next. Is that what you want?" He pushed tighter against her backside. "Yes, maybe it is. If you need to have your control stripped away to find your pleasure then you, darling, have come to the right man."

"You're insane," she cried.

In a flurry of movement, he grabbed her hands and pulled them behind her back, rendering her helpless against the onslaught of sensation his nearness created.

"Maybe. Denial does have a way of driving a person crazy." He tightened his hold until she nearly cried out from the strain.

"Damn it. I want to bite you so bad I ache with it." He flexed his hips. "Can you feel how bad?"

Spots swam in Chey's vision as her head spun out of control. Everything narrowed to the desire pulsing between her legs and the ache in her breasts for more of what he offered.

"If I do though... " He didn't have to finish the thought she knew exactly what would happen. The one thing John had known about her and always worried about was the lack of bonding between them. She'd tried to tell him what they had was enough but he'd known better. His dying words to her had said as much. Chey choked back a sob.

"I need you so bad I can't think straight, Cheyenne. Why did you have to come here? After all these years. Why now?"

Why did she come? Because Kane had implored her that Malcolm was their last hope? What did she care about their council politics? If she dug deep there were two very clear reasons she was trapped underneath Malcolm right this second. First, the trail from her husband's death led deep into the heart of cougar country and it was the only way she could get in. Second, and this was much harder to admit even to herself, she'd needed to see him again. Although the outcome had not been what she'd hoped.

Before she'd arrived, she'd managed to convince herself that what happened all those years ago meant nothing. That the only reason Malcolm had walked away from her had been because he was nothing more than an asshole using a birthmark and her heritage as an excuse to get away.

Uh huh. But John had warned you what would happen if you ever saw him again and even in death you refused to listen.

"Kane insisted no one else could lure you back. I disagreed of course but your brother can be quite insistent when he wants to be."

Malcolm dragged his teeth along the edge of her exposed neck and clamped down on her shoulder muscle. As long as she stayed perfectly still there was no chance of him breaking the skin. Seconds ticked by while he held her in his mouth like a mother would carry her cub. Her skin itched, ached with need. She fought the need to struggle, to arch into him until his teeth sank into her skin. Oh God, she craved his bite and cock something fierce.

Slowly the pressure of his teeth lessened and he lifted from her skin. "I could slide my cock into your wet pussy and bury my teeth in your flesh and you would simply scream in ecstasy."

"Malcolm, we can't do this." She cringed at the husky tone of her voice. She couldn't hide how much she wanted this.

"Shh," his hands roamed her overheated skin as he soothed her. "I only need a minute to touch. Please, baby."

Chey fought the instinct to lift her robe and spread her legs for him. The moisture flooding her sex in response to every move he made should have embarrassed her but she was way beyond that now. She wanted him so badly her mind could think of little else. Not with the hard ridge of his erection poking incessantly at her bottom.

He arched his hips and pressed deeper in between her buttocks. His fingers slipped between the fabric of the robe and stroked her thigh. The rough skin on his hand created the most delicious friction she'd ever experienced as he worked his way to the crease of her thigh.

"Can't...so bad...not good..." Her protest died on a soft gasp when he cupped her overheated center.

"Just a little more," he insisted. Before she could respond, he parted her labia and slid two fingers through the hot juices hidden between her folds.

Her brain fired into overdrive under the onslaught of sensations. Fire raced along her spine, tingling all of her nerve endings. This had to stop before she melted on the floor or they both let things go too far.

"Have to stop, Malcolm."

On a low groan, he jerked away from her, taking all of his body heat and sweet friction with him. Chey slowly eased her feet from their perch on her tiptoes and readjusted the robe around her. She fought to breathe and regain control while her body pleaded for the release it craved—at his hand. The thought of turning to face him held little appeal at the moment but staying in this vulnerable position would be even worse. She rolled to her backside and sat up, doing everything she could to avoid eye contact.

"We keep messing this up." She sighed as he forced his legs into a pair of clean jeans he'd grabbed from a drawer.

"Hell, at the moment I don't even know what *this* is. One minute we're screwing each other's brains out; the next, you're telling me you already have a mate, then we have a dead body, and then we don't, and now you no longer have a mate either. And on top of all of that, I can't stop thinking about being inside you. Fuck, Chey. My head is spinning."

Chey sucked in a deep breath. She didn't want to deal with any of this either. "We're both on overload." She pressed her hand to her now aching head and tried to sort through all the data flying by. "It's almost as if... "

"As if what?" Malcolm growled and took a step closer. "What are you thinking?"

"It's probably my own heightened paranoias." Ever since John's death she'd not trusted anyone.

"Tell me."

"All of this happening at once is almost too coincidental. Like you said, why would Kane ask for me? And if Kane didn't send Carl to follow me, then who did? There are a lot of *what if's* and *how the hell did this happen* going on. It's as if someone wants to distract us. Or me," Chey pointed out as she took a few steps to the side, putting a little more space between her and Malcolm.

"Or me."

Chey bit at her bottom lip and considered the possibilities. "Okay so if we indulge this craziness for a minute... What would someone have to gain by distracting one of us?"

Malcolm shrugged. "Hell if I know. I've been on my own for a while now just trying to deal as best I can."

"What do you mean deal? I thought you were busy living the high life out here. What, with no responsibilities to the clan and no one to tie you down, you've been positively free as a bird." The minute the words left her mouth she realized she'd just made a huge mistake.

His eyes darkened and the lethal tips of his canines poked from the sides of his mouth. "Hasn't anyone ever warned you not to poke an animal, little girl?"

The question was snarled not spoken and the vibration of it rolled over her senses, setting the hair on her skin to standing. "Don't even think about trying to scare me Malcolm Gunn. I bite back."

"Is that a promise?"

Chey rolled her eyes. She'd forgotten what an arrogant ass male kitties were when backed into a corner or refused their favorite toy. Lucky for her, it was exactly that attitude that managed to cool the lust she felt for him.

Before she could deliver her scathing retort a loud knock sounded at the door. Both their gazes flew in the direction of the sound. "What?" Malcolm demanded.

"You've had plenty of time alone. It's time to get your asses out here and finish answering our questions."

Chey scented the all too familiar smell of deceit. "He's lying."

Malcolm placed his finger over his lip, urging her to not say anything else. With her instincts screaming trouble stood outside the door, she immediately rifled through Malcolm's drawers for some clean clothes. No way did she want to face trouble in a fucking bathrobe.

"We still have to finish getting dressed."

"Don't tell him that. Jesus," she whispered.

"Get over it. But hurry and get dressed. We're going to blow this Popsicle stand. I think your theory is beginning to make sense and I have a feeling one or both of us is about to be hauled in for murder."

"What? Why?" She grabbed a pair of his sweat pants and pulled them up her hips.

"Call it a hunch." Chey watched him disappear into the closet, drawers being opened and closed the only sound he made. When he returned, her gaze was drawn to the weapons he'd strapped to his body. A gun at his hip and knives strapped to each thigh. If she'd ever doubted the man knew how to handle any situation, he was quickly proving it.

"Wait. How the hell are you going to shift like that?" She threw on a found T-shirt and tried to ignore the appreciative way he looked at her breasts.

"I'm not. But you are so hurry the hell up. If we don't get out there in five minutes or less they'll be pushing their way in here."

She wrinkled her face in confusion but they didn't have time for explanations now. Once they cleared the property and found a place to hunker down she'd demand some answers.

Malcolm slid the window open without making a sound and waved for her to go through. Without looking back she sprang through the opening and landed on her feet in the grass. So far so good. Chey surveyed the area, allowing the brief seconds she needed to focus her senses. Someone in the house was talking and judging by the muffled responses, she'd guess cell phone.

A displacement of air behind her was the only sign Malcolm had followed her out the window. She motioned to him with hand signals she knew he'd understand to apprise him of the situation. Malcolm nodded and pointed to the tree line. Seconds later, they both raced from the cabin. The only chance of a clean getaway was if they got into those trees without being spotted.

From what little of the conversation she'd picked up, Malcolm's guess had been correct. It sounded like they were preparing sedatives for them both. Boy, when she got her hands on Kane he'd be lucky to survive. None of this behavior had been expected. She'd trusted him implicitly in this situation and he'd screwed her and the brother he supposedly wanted brought home.

Lies and deceit. It seemed no one was immune.

Chey pumped her arms and legs harder and thanked her DNA for her quick reflexes. Once she shifted she'd be able to move even faster. Good considering they were about to be pursued by two pissed off animals. The bitter taste of betrayal filled Chey's mouth. Charlie was one of her kind. They were supposed to protect each other from outside clans. It was their way.

Thirty seconds from the tree line shouts and commotion sounded behind her.

"Don't look. Just move faster!" Malcolm yelled.

Chey ducked behind the first row of low bushes and scrambled to remove her clothes. Malcolm grabbed her arm.

"After you shift follow the scent of the water. Don't stop and don't waste time looking back."

"What about you?" she heaved.

"I'll meet you there. I've got what we need stashed on the other side of the river. Make it to the water and everything will be fine."

She hesitated for a second, staring into his eyes searching for answers.

"Go now." He disappeared behind the trees to her left and Chey shifted. Bones popped and muscles stretched. The pain didn't register thanks to the adrenalin coursing through her. Over the years, she'd grown accustomed to the changes her body made and barely noticed the pain. Although stress often made the shift more uncomfortable.

Fur covered her arms and legs, and in a matter of seconds she no longer looked human. She noticed the usually dormant white fur covering her limbs. The scent of the approaching cougar had made the wolf come out. The sudden sound of extra voices caught the wolf's attention. Her ears perked up.

"We're moving out now. It shouldn't take long to capture them and then we'll bring them in."

A deep rumble formed in Chey's throat during the pause. For some reason she couldn't hear the other side of the conversation.

"Yes, Sir. I won't. That's right, I tagged him."

Chey desperately wanted to hear the rest of the conversation but the scent of the woman was drawing close. It was now or never for her own escape. She crouched low and moved quickly under the brush, using the low hung branches and debris to hide her trail. They'd still scent her but she already had a plan in place to buy them a few minutes to spare.

Once she cleared the edges of brush, Chey took off at a dead run, not looking back. The colors of the forest passed her in a blur and the different scents of nature overwhelmed her. Luckily her keen sense of locating water kept her moving in the right direction. She calculated the river was less than a mile in front of her. Her mind wandered back to earlier that morning when Malcolm had lain on the ground writhing in agony. His human form more misshapen than anything she'd ever seen before. Normally when one of their kind shifted it happened almost instantaneously. His acute pain and odd formed features scared the hell out of her.

And why the hell was he out here with weapons and clothes instead of fur and muscles? Something was very, very wrong. And now that they had a band of merry council warriors on their ass it was about to turn to total shit. Chey pushed her body faster, stretching the deepest muscles of her hind legs to propel her faster than any ordinary wolf. In open territory, the cat might outrun her but the wolf knew this type of terrain much better.

About a quarter mile from her destination she turned sharply to the right and headed west for about five hundred yards before doubling back. When she returned to the point she'd originally turned from, Chey quickly shifted to cougar and leapt across two wide boulders until she could reach a solid tree branch. From there she moved tree to tree until she reached the riverbank.

Chey leapt from the thick branch she stood on to the ground thirty feet below. The moment she stopped to survey the area, she picked up on the familiar and oh so delicious scent of Malcolm. For a second her body froze, her heart pounded harder and blood rushed through her veins. His scent alone had the power to command her attention.

"About time you got here."

She whirled to face him. Protocol insisted she shift but there was something about making him see her like this that gave her too much satisfaction. She studied him carefully for any signs of offense. It probably wasn't every day he saw a white cougar. The anomaly that served as a big red flag that said, "Half breed over here." Her breath caught in her throat while she waited for his response.

"We don't have time for this. I'm sure they're not far behind. Can you cross the river? I have a vehicle hidden on the other side."

Chey nodded. She took a deep breath and sought the space inside that corralled her ability to change. She imagined it opening and allowing her human form to run free. By the time she opened her eyes the process was complete and she crouched naked at Malcolm's feet.

He grabbed her by the shoulders and pulled her up. "I don't even want to get into how much that just turned me on, baby." He nipped at her lip and released her. "Let's go."

She followed him down the steep embankment and into the cool spring water. The temperature of her body began to immediately drop.

"Hurry, Chey. I can already hear them."

Damn. Her little trick had not bought them much time at all.

Malcolm dove into the water with a splash. With powerful strokes he pulled his muscular frame across the river effortlessly. She yearned for him now more than ever. Only the voices in the distance getting distinctly louder got her moving again. Despite the lack of clothes, Chey followed him across. She didn't love swimming but she got by on just enough skill to keep her alive. The current in this part of the river was not strong thanks to the narrowing of the canyon surrounding it. Obviously Malcolm had staked this area out well in advance in case of the need for a quick getaway.

She bit her lip and stifled a grin. She found it damn hard not to admire a man that organized. It also led her down the road of too many questions. What kind of life did he lead to need this kind of preparation? Chey thought about her own various mountain hidey-holes and stashes of supplies throughout the state. Hello pot, meet kettle.

Voices behind her grew louder and Chey dipped deep for the reserves to swim faster to the shore. Malcolm climbed out of the water and over the boulders bordering the area. His biceps flexed and the water still dripping from him caught the sunlight, making his skin gleam. Her mouth watered at the sight. She followed him out of the water and scrambled across the terrain herself.

"Not much farther," he whispered over his shoulder. They were both more than aware that if they could hear their pursuers, then Ben and Charlie could hear them.

"Do I even want to know why you have an escape route already planned out?"

"Probably not." She heard the laughter in his voice and a huge grin spread across her face. The man got to her. Simple as that.

Together they ran for an unusually large clump of bushes which she discovered was where his Jeep was hidden. She moved to help him clear the way and a hard hand clamped on her arm.

"You need clothes."

The spot where his skin touched hers burned a path from her arm directly to her core. Her sex squeezed. She jerked her arm free. "Sorry, I forgot to carry some spares. Besides, we can worry about that later when we aren't about to be caught."

A growl erupted from his throat and his eyes went hard. "I don't think so." He grabbed the edge of his shirt and pulled it over his head. "This is better than nothing."

Chey rolled her eyes. "You act like you haven't already seen me naked."

"If you want anyone we run into to keep breathing, I'd suggest putting it on."

"Possessive freak," she mumbled while holding back a smile. She grabbed the shirt he held out to her and pushed it over her head. Fortunately for her it was long enough to just cover her butt; unfortunately for her, it smelled like Malcolm. Her nostrils flared and she breathed deeply.

They cleared the stacked limbs and branches from around the vehicle until they'd made an exit path.

"Cheyenne. Malcolm. Stop!"

She snapped her head around in time to see Charlie and Ben climbing over the river embankment.

"Get in now."

"Crap. I thought we had more time." She threw herself into the passenger side and barely had a chance to hang on before the engine roared to life and Malcolm raced in the opposite direction.

"We're lucky we beat Ben at all. He's the best damn tracker out there. In fact if we get away I'll suspect he's decided to let us go—for a little while."

"How can you be so sure?"

"Because I trained him and he knows how I think just as much as I know how he thinks. Our only advantage at this point is the vehicle. So hang on."

Malcolm swerved to the left and immediately to the right. Chey swore she saw a flash of fur out of the corner of her eye. Her stomach plunged to her feet. And she thought she drove crazy.

Trees sped by as they were bounced ruthlessly from their seats. With no road to follow she prayed they didn't end up in the bottom of a ditch or ravine somewhere. Death by car accident wasn't exactly in her five-year plan.

She glanced once or twice in the direction of Malcolm and found herself shocked by the hard planes of concentration across his face. That ruthless determination she'd been loath to discover stood out starkly on his ruggedly handsome face. She couldn't see his eyes but imagined them dark as midnight and as equally ruthless as the rest of him.

By the time they made it to the small park road, Chey's muscles burned from the effort of not falling out of the Jeep.

"Are they still behind us?" She swiveled to look over her shoulder. The only thing she saw was the dust in the road behind them.

"I think we finally lost them about five minutes ago. Although honestly I'm surprised. I've seen Ben on the run before and something like a Jeep on a rutted dirt road should not have outpaced him."

"You think they let us go?"

Malcolm shrugged. "Can't say one way or the other but I'm not going to look a gift horse in the mouth." He tightened his grip on the steering wheel and she watched his muscles flex as he kept the Jeep under control.

"God, is this even a road?"

"Not really. But it will do. I know these woods very well so you have nothing to worry about."

She shrugged. "Not worried." Not about the road anyway. She had bigger problems than a few potholes. Like this insane attraction to a man who couldn't stand what she was. Even after all these years, no matter how she'd convinced herself that he'd meant nothing to her she could barely sit next to him for wanting to jump him. Not to mention the scene in the woods earlier haunted her. She wanted to know what the hell that was about and as soon as they got somewhere private and quiet she would get some answers from him. One way or the other.

"So where to now? I'm not convinced yet that running was the best possible answer." She stared him down waiting for him to respond. Instead what she got was the muscle of his jaw tensing. "What? You don't seriously still think I did this?" When he remained silent, heat traveled up her face and rage formed a knot in her stomach. The bastard did. Mother Fucker.

"I don't know what to think. Before you showed up at my place this morning everything was calm and quiet. I've been minding my own business for a while now. So of course I ask myself what changed?" He turned and met her gaze, accusation clear as day. "You're what changed, sweetheart."

Rendered speechless by his accusations Chey swiveled around in her seat and stared out the open window. If that's what he really thought so be it. He'd have to get in line with the rest of her family and friends and apparently his clan as well. It seemed everyone she came in contact with had already decided she was guilty in John's death. What was another kill on top of that?

Still the pain lanced through her. As much as she tried to convince herself she didn't need someone to believe her, she'd wanted Malcolm too. Damn it. When would she learn?

Chey grabbed the seat belt and buckled herself in seconds before she pulled her knees into her chest and wrapped her arms around her legs. Her eyes slid closed and she sucked in a deep breath, taking in a fresh wave of the man who haunted her. Fate... What a bitch.

CHAPTER
TEN

S ometime later the Jeep skidded to a stop and she jerked in her seat until the seat belt caught her. Her eyes flew open and she stared through the windshield. In front of her there was a small cabin at the base of a mountain barely visible through a stand of trees. If Malcolm hadn't parked just so she probably would have looked right over it.

"Where are we?"

"Safe house. One I haven't used in a very long time so hopefully it will buy us some time to rest and grab some food before we leave again."

"Leave? You have a plan for what comes next?"

"At some point we are going to have to talk to Kane. My brother is a lot of things but disloyal isn't one of them."

Chey snorted. "You think after everything you've done he wouldn't turn on you?"

Malcolm turned to her sharply. "No I don't. If you didn't lie about him sending you here then his reasons are legit. Trust me." He pulled a duffel bag out from under his seat. "I know my brother."

Chey sniffed. She used to have blind faith like that and then John died and her family turned their back. "You might be the world's biggest fool, Malcolm Gunn. I'm not sure I want to stake my life on that."

"If you didn't kill the shifter then you have nothing to worry about. They seemed far more suspicious about my involvement. They were merely baiting you to get a rise out of me. Guess it worked." Malcolm hoisted the bag over his shoulder and headed toward the tiny cabin.

Suddenly a stab of anxiety shot through her. Alone with him she wasn't sure she could trust herself. That little bit of shut-eye had done nothing to bring her down from the shift. The animal was still too close to the surface and only one of two things helped: A lot of sleep or some intense sex. One seemed out of the question, what with them being on the run and needing to keep their guards up, and the other posed a dangerous risk to her sanity.

She could still feel the thick slide of him as he'd entered her earlier. So much had happened in the course of one day it seemed hard to believe it was just that morning. The sensations he'd elicited from her had been off the charts incredible.

"You coming?" He'd turned and now stood eyeing her warily.

"Yeah." *Although not in the way you think.* She mentally slapped herself for her wayward thoughts. She wasn't going to stay in control if she kept this up.

Malcolm punched a code into a security pad embedded into the doorframe. When the door popped open, he held it for her and waited for her to enter in front of him. Her eyes didn't need to adjust to the darkness; she could see equally well with or without light. There were many advantages to being a shifter.

Other than some basic dust on the place, it looked sparse and functional. A single couch in the one room with a table shoved in the corner. Although that table was covered with books and a rather sophisticated looking computer set up. The other side of the room functioned as the kitchen with the basic appliances and an island in the middle with two barstools. Nothing exceptional but more than adequate.

"Bathroom and bedroom are to your right. Everything else is pretty much what you see is what you get. Although around the corner is a well stocked pantry and deep freezer, so if you're hungry we should be set."

Oh she was hungry all right. Just not for food. "Another shower would be good. Don't suppose you have any extra clothes stashed here?"

"Probably not much that's going to fit. There is a dresser in the bedroom with some basic T-shirts and jeans. Maybe some boxers would work."

Chey swallowed thickly. An image of Malcolm lounging on a big bed with nothing but his boxers filled her mind. All long legs and thick muscles. She clutched her head and turned away. She'd probably turned beet red.

"You okay? That was intense back there."

"Fine." Not really. But she would be soon. "Just going for that shower." She left the room in a rush and locked herself in the bathroom. Not like a flimsy lock could keep a man like him out if he wanted in. Still, that little barrier gave her a sense of peace she desperately needed at the moment. She quickly stripped her clothes and stepped into the marginally warm water. Guess the cabin has some decent plumbing for its odd location.

She grabbed the soap and a sponge and hurriedly washed her body, ignoring the ache of her breasts or the peaks of her hard nipples begging for attention. Between her legs, the moisture of her arousal had pooled and she did her best to wash it away. She knew damn well he scented everything about her. It wasn't as if she was fooling anyone. Least of all him.

Not wanting to waste all the hot water in case he needed a shower, she turned off the spray and jumped out. She grabbed the lone towel and wrapped it around her body and went in search of some semblance of clothing that might keep her sane for the next few hours until the energy of the shift wore off.

She opened the door and Malcolm stood just on the other side. Waiting.

"What?"

"I can still smell your need. It's fucking everywhere."

She tightened her towel and set her lips in a grim line. "Big deal. You're a big boy. You can get over it."

"Just because I can't shift doesn't mean I don't feel what you do." He grabbed her hand and placed it over the hard ridge of his erection. Chey tried to ignore it, to not let him get to her. What had he said? She tried to focus on something besides the burning ache between her legs. Dammit! A shift always did this to her. Left her with adrenalin to spare and energy dying to be used. Of course, the added element of fear of trying to escape had only ramped the normal sensations to the breaking point.

"Why can't—Why can't you shift?" She could barely breathe, let alone talk, with the heat and tension filling the room, crowding her senses.

"Don't try to change the subject," he growled and licked his lips.

Oh God, those lips. She stared at them. Moist. Bitable. He wanted her as much as she wanted him. The right or wrong of it was fading fast. She met his gaze and swallowed at the hunger she recognized. The gold flecks of his eyes had spread and taken over the green color until they practically glowed. The cougar's eyes.

She wanted him. So much need. The animal under her skin clawed closer. Why did she even bother to fight it? Her heart beat faster, almost as fast as his. His nose flared, catching her scent. A low rumble began in his chest and rose to the surface.

She could do this. On her terms—her control. Chey unhooked her towel and dropped it to the floor. Naked and vulnerable she went to him.

"Don't toy with me. You won't like the results."

"Shut up." She grabbed the back of his head and pulled his mouth to hers. She kissed him with everything she felt. Hot, edgy, hungry, fierce and then some. Mouth open, her tongue sought his, desire beating a driving rhythm in her head.

He kissed her back and the taste of hunger on his tongue drove her wild. He threaded his fingers through her hair and tugged at the strands until her scalp tingled with excitement. Oh good God, she wanted him so bad.

The scent of outdoors clung to his skin, awakening every cell of her body. The smell of fresh grass, dried leaves, and the animal inside him filtered through her senses until everything pulsed incessantly. She gripped his arms tighter and pushed against him, every lean hard muscle molding to her naked form. The hard ridge of his erection pulsed at her lower abdomen. Dying for more, she rubbed against the long and thick flesh of his burning arousal.

Another growl rumbled in his throat, causing her to smile into their kiss. She loved that noise and decided it would be her personal mission to hear it as often and as much as she could. His tongue swiped against hers, sparking a moan. Already her nerve endings sizzled and she felt soft and hot inside.

Her nipples tightened and brushed against the soft hairs of his chest. Curious, her hands roamed those muscles until her fingers touched across his tiny hard points of flesh. He sucked in air and wrenched his mouth free.

"Holy hell, woman."

She grinned up at him. "What? You don't like it?"

He grabbed her hands and pinned them behind her back. His head dipped to the curve between her neck and shoulder and scraped lightly with his teeth. "I like it and you damn well know it."

She groaned at the delicious torment of his canines pushing at her skin without breaking through. He would kill her with torment like this.

"Push much more and I won't be able to go slow. Give you the pleasure you deserve."

Her head lolled back giving him more access than before. "Don't want slow," she whispered. "Can't do slow. Not after a shift." She didn't want the man, she wanted the animal inside. Rough. Hard. "Bed, Malcolm. Now. Please." Words were getting harder the more he touched her.

"I doubt you understand what you're asking for," he whispered, his breath feathering across her skin.

Her eyes popped open and met his gaze. "I know." She stared at him for a few seconds longer. "I know."

Something snapped in his gaze and she swore the gold turned downright molten. "If you change your mind, it will be too late."

Before she could respond he hauled her into his arms and moved her across the room. "Knees now."

Chey scrambled across the mattress on her hands and knees and waited. He had no idea how badly she wanted this. She'd heard the rumors. If this was the real Malcolm, then dammit, she deserved to have him. Heat gathered between her legs, making her ache more than before. Her skin itched. The animal inside rode so close to the surface she swore she felt fur sliding under the skin.

She glanced over her shoulder in time to see Malcolm shred the jeans he wore with thick claws. A hard shudder coursed through her. She wanted those hands on her, claws and all. "Hurry, Malcolm," she pleaded.

His head jerked up and he pinned her with the gaze of his beast. *Yes!*

Her claws were out, digging through the sheets and into the mattress. They'd be lucky if the room still stood by morning. The scent of her arousal filled the room. He would have caught it by now and that knowledge made her squirm. When a male shifter scented a female in heat his animal began to howl. Supposedly if it was the heat of a mate, it drove the male into a frenzy. She wanted that. It would be sublime to watch Malcolm lose the last of his prized control.

What if her combined animal scent wasn't the same... If he scented the wolf...

"Stop it."

"What?" She held her breath. He couldn't hear her thoughts.

"You're entire body just tensed up, so whatever you were thinking, stop it."

"But—"

His hand landed on her ass. A shocking slap more than a pain filled one, but it certainly caught her attention. Her back arched and a moan slipped from her mouth. Chey's lips curved in a small smile.

Thwap! She sucked in a sharp breath. That one was much stronger. The bed shifted and before she knew it, he was behind her, his thickness pushing against the flesh of her ass. She automatically shifted looking for a different touch all together.

"Don't move," he ordered.

She paused. *Was he crazy?*

A large hand, now free of claws, wrapped around her hip and pulled her tighter into his groin. Chey didn't know whether to groan or scream he felt so good. So strong. His fingers curled into the soft spot between the top of her thigh and hip and she nearly shot off the bed. Holy hell. When had that become an erogenous zone? Fuck. She could barely breathe.

He was barely doing anything to her and already the pleasure built to an impossible level. More. More.

"Cheyenne." His voice came out fractured and she felt the claws pressing into her skin.

"Don't do it. Don't you dare hold back on me, Malcolm." This time she'd kill him for it. Temporary or not, she wanted her mate.

"I don't want to hurt you."

She wrenched from his grasp and turned to face him. Her hands pressed to his face and brought him so close his harsh breaths melded with hers. "You can't hurt me. Not this time."

He winced. "I'm so sorry." The plea in his voice cracked the barrier around her heart.

Chey nipped at his jaw, stroking down his chin with her incisors. No matter what she couldn't stop touching him.

MALCOLM FELT the heat burning under her skin and it tore through his senses. The sweet rush of feminine need ripped away logic and left him without a sense of anything but her. Hunger clawed at his insides. The cat roared in his head. He wanted release and Malcolm feared this was it. He was about to lose his very long battle.

His lips covered hers and he pushed his tongue inside. Nothing else mattered. Just Chey. *Mate.*

There were so many regrets between them thanks to his carelessness with the once precious thing in his life. By rights, she should run far away from him and never return. Instead, he held her tightly and pumped his tongue between her lips relishing the sweet, sweet taste of the one woman he craved for all these years. All the things he'd tried to forget never worked. Only this eased the pain. Only her.

Unfortunately for him, the animal inside only wanted one thing. He wanted to finally possess the woman who belonged to him. To mark her. His teeth ached at the thought and when her tongue stroked over one of the tips his cock swelled and the beast roared.

He pulled back from her and stared down into her glowing eyes. He needed to show restraint but her hunger made it impossible. He curled his fingers over her breast, claws and all. He couldn't seem to control their appearance. Still, he managed to be mindful of her soft flesh. He couldn't hurt her now if he tried. She meant everything to him. She was his salvation.

He pulled her between his legs until the soft skin of her stomach cushioned his painful erection. Her resulting moan was music to his ears. With her legs parted and almost straddling his thighs, she remained open and ready for him. The sweet scent of her desire haunted him with every breath. Malcolm lifted his eyes and stared into the now midnight blue of hers and willed his racing mind to slow. To go through with this he had to ensure her pleasure. Nothing meant more. He'd rather cut off his own arm than hurt her again.

"I promise I won't leave you again," he whispered against her lips moments before he stroked their softness with his much rougher tongue. A hard shudder racked through her, making him cradle her closer. "You'll always be safe with me."

Goddess knew he'd do anything to keep these promises to her. As long as he survived. The cold reality of his situation slammed into him like a wall of ice. A shifter who couldn't shift wasn't much use to a woman like her.

She holds the key.

The dark whisper slithered through his mind. It couldn't be that simple? He shook his head. All these years of pain. He'd managed to blame everyone and everything he could think of, but not once did he think of her. Or that his own stupidity and false pride had led him here.

Take her.

He couldn't stop touching her beautiful skin. The perfection in front of him felt like a treat he didn't actually deserve but knew he'd take anyway. It was his way. It always had been. He closed his eyes and lowered his head to her neck once more. His teeth gripped the tendon, providing what he knew were tremors of uncontrollable need. For a shifter, there wasn't a more sensitive spot on their body. In return, Chey followed suit and grazed her tiny incisors back and forth across his neck a few times. With his solid grip on her, she didn't have much room to move.

So she tried something different. She wriggled her bottom on his legs and canted her hips until the head of his cock lay lodged at the wet, heated entrance of her sex. He locked his jaw and gritted his teeth against the juices spilling across the head of his shaft.

Malcolm fought to hold back. He began to question if he had the strength not to overwhelm her. His hands tightened on her waist, holding her still. He gulped deep breaths, knowing nothing would help him now.

"Malcolm." Her legs shook almost as hard as her voice.

"Oh Goddess, I know baby." He gasped at the heat burning him. "Can't think clearly."

"Screw thinking, Malcolm. I can't stand it. Just fuck me."

Hell yes! The pleasure burning at the base of his spine grew hot—unbearable. His nerve endings cried for relief. Malcolm's head fell back and the sucking wet grip of her body slid down his flesh. She moved in such exquisite slow motion he thought he would die before she took all of him inside. He snarled. Control slipped from his grasp.

"You need to know..."

On a hard stroke, Chey's tight muscles parted and sucked him inside to the base of his dick. Wet, hungry and so damn tight he couldn't breathe. She leaned forward, her mouth rubbing his shoulder again. Seeking. Before he could stop her, she sank her teeth into the sweet spot, slicing into his flesh in the most incredible sensation of pain and pleasure. A roar slipped from his mouth seconds before he latched onto the tender spot he had no business ever touching. Rational thought deserted him as his teeth sank deep. The taste and scent of her blood sent him into a frenzy.

He pushed her onto her back and pounded into her. The bed shook, and the lamp on the side table crashed to the floor. Her mouth popped free and a scream tore from her throat. The cat inside roared in response. Wild to get free. Without restrain he took and gave, thrusting in and out of the tight flesh he'd so desperately needed, all while his teeth held her in place.

Her nails dug into his arms while her body bucked ruthlessly underneath him. With the animal in charge the reality of their lives slid away. The only thing that mattered to him was his mate's pleasure, the keening cries she used to direct him and the frantic desperation for even more.

When her muscles bunched and turned vise-like around his shaft, he pumped harder. Liquid heat from his mate scorched through him, pulling at the fire of pleasure burning in his balls. A rough wave of sensation raced along his spine and exploded over his skin. He groaned into his bite on her delicate flesh and frantically licked at her skin. Mate. Mate. Mate.

His release whipped through him until she'd milked him dry. Still, shudders racked his body in aftershocks that rocked the bed. Primal pleasure beyond belief swamped his brain, building, burning until he jerked his mouth from her shoulder, and lifted his head back and the cat roared to the surface. His.

He'd been such a fool for so long. He'd only needed his mate to feel whole again. Bones popped and skin ripped. He'd known. The minute she'd entered his house he'd felt the difference, and everything leading to this moment he'd planned. He'd warned her to never come to him. If only she'd listened. He was shifting and couldn't stop it. Now she'd know. Betrayed again...

Malcolm sprang from the bed and Chey recoiled in shock. *What the hell?* Fur sprouted along his skin and he screamed in an agony that burned her sensitive ears. His shrieks of pain scared her. "Malcolm, what's happening?"

He turned and stared at her, but the eyes of the man were gone and the cat stared back. His lips peeled back from his teeth. Warning her.

This was like no shift she'd ever seen before. The sound of a bone breaking caught her attention when his leg jerked underneath him. He toppled onto his face. The cry of pain coming from him scared the shit out of her. Her fear clogged her throat and the animal rose to protect her. Not her cat though. Like it or not, the wolf was stronger. In an instant, her skin disappeared and gave way to the fur. Her bones popped and stretched and the wolf arrived.

The instant she turned, Malcolm turned and hissed, still writhing on the floor. She whined. The pain etched on his face tore at her insides. The scent of his agony filled the room. Another bone popped and his arm shifted. More fur as his body gave way to the change. His mouth opened wide on a long, loud yowl and the rest of the cat emerged. Black, sleek and even larger than she remembered.

He turned to face her. His back arched and the fur on his body stood on end. He growled low and bared his teeth. Damn cat. He still hated the wolf. Pain lanced through her heart. Even now he wouldn't accept the two sides of her. For two seconds, she had half a mind to attack and give him the ass kicking he so deserved. All this mate bullshit he'd been feeding her... She'd begun to believe. Maybe even a small part of her had hoped he'd help her and they'd... She paused. What? Live happily ever after? She growled in return and shifted back to the woman.

"I thought you couldn't shift?" She jumped off the bed and stalked to the chest of drawers in the corner. Time to get dressed and get as far away from him as possible. She found a pair of black sweat pants and an old T-shirt in the bottom drawer and yanked them out. Her first stop would have to be for some real clothes. Something that actually fit her. She shoved her legs into the sweats and mentally cursed herself up one side and down the author. Stupid fool.

"You need to let me explain." She tripped at the sound of his voice. Still more animal than man. With reluctance she turned and faced him after she swiped the shirt over her head. Sweat covered his body and his chest heaved with the effort to breathe.

"Why? So you can lie to me some more?"

"I didn't lie. My ability to shift has been diminishing for years and only a handful of times in the last few months have I managed it." His hands swiped the hair from his eyes. Emotions swam in the green pools of his gaze but damned if she could decipher them. Much like the cat, he was an enigma. Supposedly he shouldn't even exist.

"So what? Now you're cured?"

"I don't know what I am. Other than hot, exhausted and edgier than I've ever been in my life. If you were a smart woman you'd run out of here right now." The resignation in his voice alarmed her.

She glanced over him from head to toe. There were no signs of the cougar other than the shredded sound of his voice and the faint glow around the rim of his eyes.

The muscles in his body still twitched, drawing her gaze to the thick cock lying heavy between his thighs. Despite the mind blowing orgasm mere minutes ago, the shift had aroused him again. She sniffed the air, searching beyond the obvious desire. Nothing. Dammit!

"What aren't you telling me?" She pressed her hand to her head. "Something isn't right. I can sense it. Something other than your cat being repelled by my wolf."

"I wasn't repelled."

There! The pungent odor of a lie. "Don't fuck with me, Malcolm."

He sighed and bent over and grabbed his jeans. He'd barely pulled them up before he continued. "You caught me off guard is all. It's still something I have to get used to."

"You've had years to get used to it," she accused.

He pushed his fingers into his hair and blew out a hard breath. "You know what I mean."

"What else? There's more, I can feel it. Just spit it out already." The look of agony on his face gave him away. Her stomach flipped and clenched.

"Ever since I picked up your scent, something changed. I changed."

She crinkled her forehead, not understanding.

"In the forest this morning. With your scent in my head, the cat crawled under my skin demanding freedom. Despite the agonizing pain I was so close... "

"What do I have to do with that?" Her head began to spin. She had a sick feeling in the pit of her stomach where he was going with this.

"All these years. Do you have any idea how close to feral I'd become? I've done things. Things I can never be forgiven for. And then there you were. Practically an offering on a platter, the missing piece to the puzzle. I simply needed my mate."

Chey shook her head. Took a few steps back. This wasn't happening. "No."

"Apparently yes."

She whipped around to face away from him. *Run, Chey. Run.* He'd known from the moment she'd stepped in his house. That's why he'd been so frantic to claim her. He only wanted her for what she did for his body chemistry. He wanted a fucking chemical reaction, not a mate. It had nothing to do with her. Tears threatened and she swiped them away. He wasn't worth it. He'd called it from the beginning. They were too different. She didn't fit in his world and he certainly didn't fit in hers. Apparently no one did.

"Say something."

Chey choked back a sob. He'd used mating heat against her. The moment they were alone he'd pounced. And she'd let him. No, she wasn't about to deny her part in all of this. Mating had been in the back of her mind since she'd gotten the call from Kane. Along with Malcolm's warning all those years ago.

Don't ever let me see you again. You won't like it.

Truer words have never been spoken.

Mate.

She wanted to kick herself. No, she wanted to kick him and run away. It would be so easy. Just walk out the door and disappear. She'd never have to see him again. Hesitantly, she took another step in the direction of the door.

"Don't even try it. I'll find you. That's if you can get away."

She whirled back at him, rage filling her. "Don't you dare tell me what I can and can't do. You bastard."

"That's your bastard now." The arrogance stamped on his features infuriated her.

"Why you—" Chey breathed in slowly. Even with the rage boiling through her blood, fighting wasn't going to get them anywhere. She had her own agenda by coming here and if this is what it took, so be it.

"Cheyenne, I didn't know anything for sure."

"But you were willing to gamble with the rest of my life for yours." It wasn't a question and she prayed he stayed silent. Her lips trembled. The situation had definitely spun out of her control and she needed to find a way to get it back. She still had a traitor to find.

"Chey." He whispered her name and she flinched. For a few crazy moments, he'd given and she'd taken the greatest pleasure of her life. Now she ached. To her embarrassment part of that ache was centered in her sex. She'd want him for the rest of her life. They were now tied together. If and when she walked away this time it would be to no one else. There would be no John to pick up the pieces to save her from a broken heart.

She jerked in surprise at her own thoughts. Her heart already ached. She might have to live with unrequited feelings for a man who didn't deserve her, but that didn't mean she had to let him control her body or her emotions. He could kiss her ass if that's what he thought.

"You're even crazier than they say you are."

Malcolm shrugged. "Whatever works. That's been my motto for years."

His obvious indifference ate at her resolve. It would be so much easier if she could just walk out that door and never return. Although she didn't doubt he would hunt her relentlessly. If his body burned even half as much as hers there would be no stopping him. He was a black cougar after all. The most savage of them all. And he thought wolves were bad. She scoffed.

"What about the people after us? Do you have a plan for getting out of that mess?"

"Actually I do. I'm going home."

"What?" she sputtered. "So you can be tossed in a cell and then tried by the council?" He moved close. Too close. His hand touched her jaw.

"You keep forgetting that they're not sure which one of us is guilty."

"Then it wouldn't be that difficult for them to hang us both. I can't believe you're going to be this naïve. Can't you see what's been going on practically under your own nose?"

Malcolm eased back on the bed but not before snagging her around the waist and bringing her down with him. He rubbed his nose in her neck and inhaled deeply. She struggled to get out of his arms and he tightened his hold. His arm banded around her in an unbreakable bond. Tired of her fruitless efforts, Chey stilled under his hand. The more she rubbed on him the more she became aroused. As did he if the hard erection poking at her hip was anything to judge by.

"Let me up."

"No."

She sighed. "You're a pain in the ass."

He chuckled, a deep sound she felt in his chest. "Are you really just figuring that out?"

For months, Chey had been hunting, with every clue leading her closer to Malcolm. Or at least his family. Someone close to them had to be responsible, but she hadn't figured out who or why.

"Are you going to tell me what's got your brain in such a twist?"

"I didn't murder John." She spoke quietly waiting for his reaction. Other than the slight tension she felt in his muscles, he remained silent. "But someone definitely did."

"I'm not sure you want to talk about this with me. Me thinking about another man with you is a very bad image at the moment."

Chey rolled her eyes. The poor alpha male always had to beat his hands on his chest. *Me man. You woman. Do what I say and shut the fuck up.*

She bit her lip to keep from laughing out loud at that image. Oh boy this was not going to be easy but maybe it would be fun after all. She could sure take him down a peg or two.

"Anyways, as I was saying... I've spent the past year quietly trying to find the killer."

Malcolm sat up and lifted her from his lap. She settled at the opposite end of the bed from him and waited for him to say something. Anything.

"And?" His eyebrows quirked. She definitely had his attention now.

"The few sparse clues I can piece together led me to your clan. A few random phone calls, a couple of tattered receipts. It's all very circumstantial but my gut tells me I'm headed in the right direction. And then out of the blue Kane calls me. That was about the last damn thing I expected. You told your brother about me?"

"I might have mentioned it one night over a few too many beers." He shrugged. "No big deal. I doubt I shared much."

"You don't even remember?" A fresh wave of anger crashed into her. The callous bastard.

"Look, Chey. I made a huge mistake. I get that now. But you don't understand what not being able to shift does to a man. It's like being eaten alive from the inside out. The cat wanted free and I couldn't let him. No matter what I tried. You have any idea what that does to your sanity?"

"Excuses, Malcolm. That's all I'm hearing. But dammit that's beside the point. Let me finish."

He waved his hand and leaned back.

"I think whatever is going on this goes beyond one murder. Well, two now if you consider the shifter today. Don't you find it odd that the only enforcers the clan has are systematically being removed from the clan? First you. Then Lucas and now Kane's job is threatened."

He raised his eyebrows.

"Yeah. I know all about Kane's mate." Her stomach turned at the memory of the pictures that had been delivered to her house. That's when she'd finally faced the truth. She was not over Malcolm and likely never would be. John had sensed the truth, and mere days later, she'd found him stabbed in the chest. He'd managed to tell her that he'd only been trying to protect her before he gave in. She'd later learned that the knife had nicked an artery near his heart. There'd been no time to save him before he bled out.

"At least I didn't try to mate with her."

Chey recoiled at the insult. Pain sliced through her chest and guilt threatened to overwhelm her. She clenched her jaw to hold back any further insults. This conversation would go exactly nowhere if neither of them kept their cool. "Getting back to my point. There seems to be a shit storm surrounding you and your brothers and it seems like everyone connected to you is getting swept up in it."

"Could be coincidence. We aren't all that close anymore."

"I don't believe in coincidences. Do you?"

"Not really."

"Can you remember when exactly things in your family began to fall apart?"

Malcolm scrubbed his hands over his face and pushed out a rough breath. "I don't know. It's been so long."

"Okay, let's do this." Cheyenne jumped up and began rifling through drawers until she came across a pad of paper and pencil. She returned to the bed and sat next to him. "I'll ask questions and you answer the best you can. I have a hunch we're onto something."

"Maybe."

"Let's create a timeline. When you met me, were you and your brothers still close?"

"Sort of. We were all still working as enforcers but the tension between us had grown tight by then. After our mother left, things were hard but then when Dad died, no one seemed to care that much anymore. I spent nearly all of my time out by the border leaving Lucas and Kane to deal with council politics. I never did have much stomach for that kind of thing."

She nodded and wrote all of his information down. "But you were all still together. What happened after you left me?"

Darkness clouded his eyes. A bright pang of regret bloomed inside her. They were never going to get past their mistakes if they didn't stop revisiting them. She laid down her pencil and angled her body closer. "I'm only asking for the purpose of getting to the bottom of this. I really don't want to keep hashing out the past. What's done is done and can't be changed." Not when she had the here and now to obsess over. He'd tricked her again and she wasn't about to let him off the hook. But finding John's killer was more important than revenge on Malcolm at the moment.

"I was an idiot. I can admit it. But dammit, Chey what I did was for the best for both of us. Neither one of us knew what we were getting into."

She'd known. She'd been young, not stupid. "Let's just get through this, okay?"

He nodded. She grabbed the pad of paper and scribbled some more notes.

"So after..."

"I tried to immerse myself in work but it wasn't enough. My emotions were all over the map and that translated into a lot of rage. So I lashed out." He hesitated. "I'm not sure you want to hear this."

Probably not. "Go ahead. I doubt you can tell me something I haven't already heard. I don't know how or why, but news about you filtered its way to me on a regular basis. It was as if no matter where I went I couldn't get away from it."

His expression darkened. "Someone knew you were my mate."

Chey almost laughed out loud. "Do you know how ridiculous that sounds?"

"What? That someone knew?"

"No. I don't know. I mean just the actual part about being your mate. Aren't we both getting a little old for this predestined, you can only be with one person crap?"

He glared at her. "I'm going to pretend you didn't say that."

"Pretend away." She grabbed the notepad and pencil again and began doodling in the corner. This whole damn thing was like a puzzle and her brain kept circling without quite landing on the missing puzzle piece. Maybe he was on to something. It would explain a lot of the weird things over the years.

"You've been outcast, Lucas is not currently welcome in the clan and Kane is having trouble holding onto his guardianship..." Her thoughts swirled and her mind swam. "What happens when there aren't any black cougars left?"

Malcolm shrugged. "Not sure. No one's even contemplated that until now as far as I know. What were the odds all of us would end up breaking some fundamental laws in the span of a few years? I'm sure the council must have some sort of plan."

"What the hell kind of plan could replace the three of you? Your presence keeps the balance among all the clans. They fear you."

"Yeah, intimidation goes a long way." His sarcasm wasn't lost on her nor was the bitter tone in his voice.

"It's the animal genetics and you know it. The wolves don't like the cats, the cats want nothing to do with the wolves and no one wants to be near the psychics because they make us nervous." She tapped the pencil on the paper. Sifting through all of the possibilities. "So far nothing makes sense, and if there's one thing I've learned over the past few years, it is that if it doesn't seem logical then it has to be personal. Someone is up to something, and whatever it is, I'd say you and your brothers are at the core of it, and of course anyone who stands in the way of his or her goal."

"What are you saying?" His eyes narrowed.

Chey blew out a frustrated breath. "Jesus, Malcolm. I don't know. My head hurts, I'm tired and I'm feeling a little desperate to figure this out. I've been hunting too long." She closed her eyes and rubbed her forehead. She wasn't about to tell him everything. But being this close to him after they'd... There must be something wrong with her. She certainly needed her head examined.

He reached for her and she jerked out of reach just in time.

"What the hell, Chey?"

"We aren't doing that again," she warned. "You used me. Although after seeing the physical agony of what you've gone through, I can't say I actually blame you. In your situation I'd probably do the same."

"No, you wouldn't. That's not the kind of woman you are. You would never do something to someone you care about that would hurt them. That's the difference between us."

Chey tried to filter through his words to the emotions underneath and failed. Whatever feelings fueled his thoughts he'd managed to carefully conceal behind his schooled features. Wasn't that exactly what she'd heard about the black cougars? Their genetics were different. The animal kept a little more of the control over the human side. Not like she had any room to talk. She had DNA soup that made her an outcast. Even among their own kind, they remained wary with each other. Trust was never easily given. Ever.

He reached for her again and this time she allowed it. She was simply too tired to fight with him. Her body still simmered with an arousal she had no idea how long she could fight. Where Malcolm had left off the explanation of a born mate when he'd walked away, John had picked up the slack. There were a lot of prophecies involving the rare phenomena but most of what they had to go on was pure rumor.

"Lay down and sleep. We'll be safe here for a few more hours before we have to move on." His fingers rubbed her arm. A motion she took an unreasonable amount of comfort in.

Like it or not, their genetics already tied them together. He just had no idea how much. Chey curled on her side, a shiver working through her.

"Cold?"

"Always." The bed dipped beneath her and a few seconds later Malcolm placed a blanket over her.

"I'm going to check the perimeter. There are safeguards in place but I'd feel a hell of a lot better if I confirmed no other signs of visitors."

She nodded. Letting their guard down now would be foolish, but she was so damn cold she ached. She didn't want him to leave her. Irrational fear crowded her mind. His body heat would warm her. If only...

The air in the room shifted, grew colder with his departure. Exhausted from the stress of these long months, she grabbed the edge of the blanket and hunkered deeper into the softness. Her mind wandered through the day's events. Had it really only been one day? It seemed like an eternity ago she'd broken into his house more determined than ever for information that would help her find the man who'd killed John. Like it or not, his death was her fault. She'd gotten involved with Malcolm against her better judgment—fallen in love with him actually. Then, when he'd lived up to his reputation, she'd allowed John to help her. Chey cursed her nature and her damned shifter DNA.

Now what? If she wanted Malcolm to help her find some answers then she needed to tell him the truth. At least then he wouldn't be so anxious to call her mate. What she'd done... At least, what she'd perceived as a betrayal all those years ago had been honest. Brutal but honest. He hated the wolf. Probably still did. The hurt of the cat's reaction earlier still stung.

Suddenly, heat blanketed her. Through the haze of near sleep she realized it was Malcolm, and he was both naked and aroused. Thank God for the clothes she'd opted to leave on. She doubted she could have resisted him pressing to her flesh-to-flesh. Moisture gathered between her legs.

"Malcolm." She whispered his name into the dark, felt him stiffen then relax again.

"Shh. Just sleep, baby. You need the rest. It's going to be a rough day tomorrow."

"I need to tell you something." She trembled with wariness, so afraid of his reaction to what she needed to confess. The silence between them stretched on until his breathing evened out behind her and she wondered whether or not she'd even said the words out loud.

How well did she know the man who'd decided to lay claim to her? They'd both changed over the years. So much bitterness stood between them. She could have told him the truth long before now, maybe even saved John if she'd just been more honest. Her fault.

Malcolm moved, startling her from her wayward thoughts. He draped a leg over hers and curled his arm around her stomach, his erection nudging insistently against her skin. How he slept in that condition she couldn't fathom. Talk about distracting and uncomfortable. She was about to turn over and confront his arousal when the soft sound of a snore pushed air through her hair. Chey had to bite her lips to hold back a laugh. She lay there tense, waiting for him to move again. When he didn't, her exhaustion took over and she closed her eyes. Sleep dragged her down. In the morning she'd tell him. She needed a full night's rest to deal with that kind of anger.

Heat surrounded him. The kind of comforting warmth he hadn't experienced in a very long time. For the first time in practically as long as he could remember, he hadn't woken filled with the pain of the cat trying to claw its way out. Even crazier, the slight rumble coming from his chest sounded suspiciously like a purr.

That he felt happy and renewed should have been his first clue that his situation was about to go to shit. Any time he'd ever let his guard down there was always someone there ready to kick him in the teeth. He opened his eyes and stared into the sleeping face of the one woman who had the power to ruin his life. Her blonde hair tumbled wildly around her head, almost the same color as her luminescent skin. That coloring gave her the appearance of fragility, something he knew to be almost laughable. She'd almost kicked his ass on a couple of occasions.

Sanity finally penetrated his sleep-fogged brain and he realized his throbbing dick was wedged between her thighs, nudging at her very slick pussy. The scent assailed his brain, making his heart pound harder and his breath quicken. Raging need shot through him, robbing him of even a shred of common sense. How in the hell had they ended up like this? And more importantly... How was he going to resist taking this too far before she woke up?

His hand clenched her thigh in an effort to stop from going any further. Yet his hips bucked at that moment, pushing his tip firmly against her entrance. One quick thrust and he'd be buried in all that beautiful silken heat he loved so damn much. She had a magic pussy. How else could he explain the need his brain couldn't override? Damn.

Malcolm curved his hand around her ass cheeks and considered shifting them apart. Fuck that. The sensation of her sweet cream coating his aching flesh nearly made his mind numb with pleasure. Suddenly he had to taste her. He'd give anything to slide his tongue between those soft lips and nibble on her hard little clit until she begged him for mercy. He inwardly groaned. The images of her tender flesh in his face wasn't helping the situation at all. Somewhere in the back of his mind the sensible man poked at him to move the fuck away. Thank goodness he could shut *him* the hell up.

"Chey," he whispered into her ear seconds before untangling their limbs. He swallowed tightly against the friction the slightest move created. Pleasure exploded through his mind. He ground his teeth together to keep from shouting out. It amazed him how much effect she had on him. Mind numbing really.

Mate. The single word echoed in his mind. He already knew how much he didn't deserve her, yet nothing could stop him from possessing her. Not even the wolf. A momentary hesitation stilled him. The cat stretched, a mewl of protest in the back of his brain. He growled in response. Fuck the wolf. He was so fucking far from perfect, what did it matter who her parents were? He'd become an outcast. Even worse, a criminal. He'd kidnapped his own brother when he couldn't take the pain a second longer.

Now he'd suffer for not telling her his suspicions yesterday when her appearance made him feel more energized than ever before. Half his brain had been focused on testing his theory while the other had been consumed with the need for his mate. Years of denial had exploded in an instant and the information about another man had nearly sent him over the edge. He'd been hell bent on killing something for a while there yesterday.

She moved again, bringing her beautiful, hard-tipped breast directly into his line of sight. His mouth watered. Resistance flitted in his mind almost as fast as it departed. Controlling his lust in the face of so much temptation would be impossible for any man, but especially one like him. He always liked his women compliant but enjoyed a good fight to get them there. He'd considered for half a second tying her to his bed and having his way with her, but there was only so far he could take this at the moment. He wanted to give her an incredible amount of pleasure, not get killed.

On a regretful sounding sigh, she rolled onto her back, splaying her legs in a way that easily opened her to him. The scent of her arousal grew stronger. His mouth watered.

"Damn it, Chey. Wake up." He kissed her lips and cursed the need to take riding him harder than before. He didn't expect that biting her, tasting her blood would drive him this mad. He blazed a trail of kisses from her mouth to the gentle curve of a breast, where a couple of well-placed nips to the soft flesh made her writhe against him.

"Mmm," she murmured without opening her eyes. "Do you make a habit of undressing women in their sleep?"

"I have no idea what you're talking about. You were like this when I woke up." Practically of its own volition, his tongue peeked out and stroked across the tight flesh of a nipple. When she didn't protest, he did it again and again until the whimpers of need falling from her mouth joined with the arching of her back. "Makes me wonder what you were thinking about all night long." He moved back and forth between breasts, making sure to share his attentions equally when finally her lids fluttered open and she nailed him with a heated gaze.

"You don't exactly play fair, do you?"

"No such thing as fair," he mumbled before scraping lightly across her nipple with his teeth.

She hissed and thrust her hips in the air. His hand pressed against her mound, the heat of it threatening to start a fire within him. They both held their breath until he eased a finger through the delicate folds that were slick with her juices.

"God, Malcolm. What's wrong with me? I feel like I'm on fire," she gasped.

"You're not the only one, babe." The craving to taste her cramped his balls until he couldn't take it anymore. He rose over her and teased her sex with his iron hard shaft.

"Oh fuuuuck. Why are you teasing me?" Her keening cries only added fuel to the already out of control fire consuming him. His limbs shook with the need to plunge inside her. To sink balls deep and not stop. He dug deep for even an ounce of control. Not like this. Not yet. He wanted to taste her. Brand her again.

"I can't stop now."

Her eyes widened. "Stop? I'll kill you if you do."

Malcolm wasn't about to remind her that she'd said no only a few hours ago. Now, as he stared into those crystal blue eyes, he knew there was no chance of turning back. She'd likely damn him later but not until she stopped screaming and begging from the pleasure he intended to give her.

"I'm going to put my mouth on your pussy until you scream, Chey. I want to feel all that sweet cream flowing across my tongue as you come for me. Are you ready for that?"

She whimpered and nodded. He smiled and eased the rest of the way down to her body where she parted her legs wide for him. He settled between her lush thighs and positioned his face over the blush pink folds that were flush with her need. The sight made the cat scream. He tried to tighten the leash and the cat shook him off. He wanted nothing to do with Malcolm's control. He kissed her first. A soft touch just above her mound. He watched her gasp and whine as he continued, making sure that every inch of delicate skin between her thighs received an equal amount of attention.

With his fingers, he parted her folds and admired the wet flesh underneath. With his head swimming from the scent alone, he swiped his tongue from one end to the other, adding a hard little flick to her most sensitive bundle of nerves. She jerked underneath him, forcing him to grip her hips with his hands to keep her in place.

"Holy hell, baby. You're so hot and sweet I might come before I ever get inside you," he whispered, trying to ignore the harsh graveled tone of his voice.

"Oh, God. More. Please. More." Her pleas did not fall on deaf ears. He smiled, more than happy to oblige her. He wanted to eat her night and day. Screw food. He needed Chey pussy for breakfast every morning.

"Relax, Chey. Let me show you how much I love every inch of you. Trust me." He immediately stroked and lapped at her sex. Touch after touch, he drove her closer to release. With her wild jerks and frantic hip thrusts he once again contemplated the ropes. She'd look so fucking good tied up. At his mercy. Begging for more all day long.

She spread her thighs wider and he stifled a smile against her thigh. That was more like it. Less fighting, more fucking. That would definitely be his motto from here on out. He licked and sucked some more, nearly exploding when she reached up and grabbed her own nipple. She rolled it between her fingers and pinched it hard.

A greedy grip of need had him plunging his tongue inside the entrance of her tight and clenching pussy. He worked his magic until she whimpered and cried out for relief. A wide smile spread across his face while he worked her relentlessly. How many times had he dreamt of her? Of this? The reality was easily a hundred times better. He'd been such a damned fool. He growled in warning when she grabbed his hair and tried to direct him where she so desperately needed him. Her hold eased.

"I can't take it," she cried.

Malcolm had no intention of torturing his mate a second longer. He curled his tongue around her clit and sucked on the plump bud he knew would give her the release she sought. Her thighs tightened around his head, his claws shredded the sheets and her whimpers filled the room. The center of her body flowed hot and liquid. She was so close.

One last pull and she arched violently, screaming in orgasm. A sudden jerk brought her off the mattress and Malcolm raced to catch her before she fell off the bed. He grabbed her arms and pulled her to him. Her heart raced wildly against his chest, her breathing ragged in his ear. Her head fell onto his shoulder and the world beyond the two of them melted away. The tremors still running through her squeezed his heart. He ignored the insistent throbbing in his cock and instead focused on the incredible moment presented to him. His woman in his arms, holding onto him like a lifeline. She made everything worth it.

Her nails bit into his arms, making him smile. He lowered his mouth to the red spot on her neck where he'd marked her earlier. Moments before his mouth closed over the sensitive skin, she murmured his name. He bit down.

CHEY'S common sense was screaming at her. *Don't do this. Not again.* However, the aftermath of her explosive release left her unable to think straight. Like it or not, she wanted more and anything less wasn't enough. A fresh wave of ecstasy from his mouth on her shoulder washed over her, pulling her deeper into the desire she couldn't wipe away no matter how hard she tried.

With his teeth embedded in her flesh, his hot tongue stroked over her again and again. The man knew how to use his mouth, that's for sure. Her entire body felt hot and loose under his touch despite the frantic way she held onto him. That skin-to-skin contact meant everything to her. Hell, it was more than the contact. Had a day ever gone by she hadn't thought of him? She'd spent a lot of time and energy on being angry with him instead of trying to move on.

One of his hands roamed to her thigh and spread her legs until she straddled him. It would be so easy to lift up and take him inside her. Her stomach jerked at the remembered sensation of his thick shaft pushing its way inside her. She wanted to feel that again but not yet. First, she needed her own exploration.

She pushed at his shoulders with no results. He was like a brick wall. "Malcolm." She shoved again.

In a slow, sort of regretful motion, he released her shoulder and looked into her eyes. *Wild.* That's the only word she could think of when she looked into the golden green of his gaze. The primal hunger she recognized took her breath away. He wanted *her.*

"I've never wanted a woman the way I want you." His confession shocked her. He'd been with so many others. She hated that all the stories she'd heard plagued her still. Her eyes closed and she turned away from his knowing eyes.

"Look at me." His hand curved around her jaw and firmly turned her back to face him. "Open your eyes, Chey."

She shook her head. "Don't want to."

"Yes you do. Look at me," he repeated. The commanding tone of his voice made it all but impossible not to obey. Her heart ached for him.

"The last few years have been more difficult than you can imagine." Tears formed in her eyes and threatened to fall. Somehow she held back.

"I only want you. That's all that matters. If nothing else, please don't underestimate how much I desire you." He lifted her hand and brought it to his thigh, where her fingers brushed his erection. "Feel how hard you make me. How much I need you. If you believe nothing else, believe that I am yours every bit as much as you are mine."

Chey tried and failed to swallow past the lump forming in her throat. He made it difficult for her to catch her breath.

"You walked away and never looked back. I didn't do this." Not once had he tried to contact her. If he had, things might have turned out very different. This fantasy he had about her now wouldn't last. Not once he found out the whole truth.

"I never said I wasn't a cold hearted bastard. But a man can only take so much and I've reached my limit." He dragged his thumb across her lip. "My methods have always been harsh but back then my motives weren't complicated. I had a duty I owed to my family. The rules I resented were still rules and it was all I had left to cling to. Funny how quickly all that turned. Now I'm prepared for any outcome except one."

She looked at him, holding her breath while waiting for him to continue.

He pressed his lips to hers for a gentle kiss. "If you walk away now it's nothing less than I deserve but for now I have hope."

Chey trembled under the liquid gold of his gaze. For a fleeting moment, he gave her hope as well. The dark, haunting emotions she carried with her on a daily basis slid to the deep recesses of her mind. Right here in this moment, she believed her world hadn't turned upside down and ripped her heart out.

"It's impossible to change the mistakes of the past. You can never go back and undo what was done."

"I know. So that leaves only now and what we choose to do with the future." He brushed his hand down her arm, soothing her.

"If only it were that easy." He had no idea what he had in store for him if she stayed with him much longer. The truth always went for the jugular.

"Stay with me today. Worry about tomorrow later." He cut off her protest by kissing her again. A soft slant of lips across hers, a swift plunge of his tongue into her mouth until the heat exploded in her senses and he got exactly what he wanted: her need.

She grabbed at his chest and arms, clawing her way to his waist. The inward hiss against her mouth only spurred her on. The press of his cock at her tender flesh sent shockwaves streaking through her. As much as she wanted him inside her, slaking both their need, there was something she had to have first. It was her turn to blow his mind.

Chey placed both palms on his chest and pushed with all the strength she could muster. Fortunately for her, catching him off guard worked perfectly. He fell back on the bed with a dull thud and a quizzical expression on his face.

"Chey... What are you doing?"

Trying to catch her breath. His movement caused the head of his dick to press against her clit and a harsh burst of pleasure had exploded over her. She gulped air until the fog in her brain dissipated. Finally, she slowly lifted her hips until their bodies no longer touched.

A warning growl erupted from Malcolm.

"Let me do this my way this time. I need this. Please."

The harsh expression on his face softened and he nodded, although the muscle tic in his jaw indicated he allowed this with the barest of control. She liked that. It gave her the impression of power, something that had been lacking in her life for quite some time.

"I've dreamt of this you know. You lying in my bed with me hovering over you. Touching every single inch of your body."

His teeth clenched and those rumbling growls returned. "I love that sound you know. I don't know what it is about your growls but they make me so wet."

"Jesus, Chey. How am I supposed to lie here after a comment like that?"

She laughed, surprised to hear the unfamiliar sound from her own mouth. How did he keep doing that to her? "Come on, Malcolm. Be a good little kitty for me."

"I'm about to show you a good little kitty." The words were rough—the tone all deep, dark need. A shiver worked over her.

Chey ignored him and curled against his side until her face was only inches away from his groin. His erection was thick, the engorged head a deep shade of red with a tinge of purple. She wrapped her fingers around the shaft and lifted it from his stomach. Pre-cum glistened at the top, beckoning her. She had to taste.

Chey brought her lips to the tip and flicked her tongue across the small slit at the top. Salt and spice exploded across her taste buds, awakening her senses even further. Bold now, she squeezed her hand until he hissed his appreciation. Control. She liked this. She circled the head and lapped at every spot of flesh she could touch. She loved the soft, smooth as silk skin stretched taut from his desire.

"Ahhh, Chey. You plan to kill me today don't you?" His fingers slid into her hair and tightened enough to tug her forward. She followed his direction and covered his head completely. The insistent ache between her thighs nearly drove her mad while she took him nice and slow. They didn't have to rush. She had time to explore him and that's what she aimed to do.

How many nights had she lain in bed and dreamed about this? Despite all the changes she'd gone through, it was brief memories of the cougar who played with her and the man who'd taken her virginity that got her through the roughest days. She'd managed to nurse the anger only for a few months. How did you stay mad at the man who'd given you the greatest gift of your life? Instead, it was the emotional pain that had lingered despite everything.

His muscles tightened and he sucked in a sharp breath. "I don't think I have the control for this for long, baby. You're killing me. I'm going to crawl out of my skin if you don't let me inside you."

Instead of slowing her movements, Chey picked up the pace. Him in control was exactly what she didn't want. The thought of him under her control or, better yet, completely out of control, made her stomach clench with excitement.

A dangerous growl she recognized all too well filled the room. "When you get done playing, I'm going to fuck you. I'm going to flip you on your stomach and hold you down while I take you until we're both in the agony you're giving me."

His whispered words worked over her like warm oil on cold skin. Her legs trembled and her stomach fluttered wildly. She wasn't exactly immune to the clawing animal inside. She screamed in her head for more until Chey thought she would go out of her mind.

"Fuck. Stop." The alarm in Malcolm's voice shocked Chey to the core. She lifted her head and he launched from the bed. "We've got incoming."

"What? How? Who? Are you sure?" She reached for her clothes and began to dress.

"Don't bother. We're going to have to make a run for it."

She only hesitated for a second before she shoved the pants back down her legs and stepped out of them. It didn't take a genius to know he meant they'd be shifting soon.

He grabbed her hand and dragged her to the ground. "Stay low. I have no idea if they're coming in hot."

"Who? What the hell is going on? How could anyone find us here?"

"The who is likely Ben and that bitch. The how I have no idea. Only a couple of people know about this place."

"How much time do we have before they're at the house?" They didn't have time to worry about how they'd been found. For now, their complete focus had to be on getting the hell out of here without getting captured.

"Less than a minute or two. They're right out front. Hence we aren't getting out of here in the Jeep. I'd bet money on it being disabled as we speak. But we can't shift until we get clear of the house so we've got to go now. I can get us out of here but you have to stay close."

Chey smirked. "Just go. I'm right behind you."

He squeezed her hand and planted a hard kiss on her lips before letting go. The look in his eyes made her stomach tumble. He had way too much power over her. Before she could think about that her ears perked up. Quiet scrapings at the front door. "They're here."

Malcolm crossed his mouth with his finger halting their conversation. If the people out front were shifters they'd be able to hear every word they said. For once, her incredible hearing would be working against her.

Moving from the bedroom she followed Malcolm into the shadows of the large living and kitchen area. The windows were not covered and if they weren't extremely careful they'd become sitting ducks. All of their senses were stronger than humans, including their eyesight. She could see in the dark nearly as well as the daylight. Already she began debating which animal to allow free. She'd been told many times how weird it was that she could be either. That in one body she captured both the spirit of the wolf and the cougar. Natural enemies.

It didn't feel weird to her. How could it? She'd known nothing else. Each one had their advantages and disadvantages, but in a time sensitive situation it wasn't easy enough to go back and forth. During the precious seconds it took to change she would be incredibly vulnerable. The wolf was always stronger in a fight but the cougar moved much faster.

Malcolm moved again and she followed. So far the intruders had not been able to breach the door. He led her to what she thought had been a simple pantry to find the far corner held a trap door. Malcolm lifted the door and she peered down the steps leading under the house. When he indicated for her to go, she hesitated. Trapped under the house didn't sound like a good idea.

Malcolm placed his mouth right at her ear and barely whispered, "Trust me."

Trust him. Boy, wasn't that a tall order. However, she did believe in his own need for self-preservation enough to believe he wasn't going to get them caught. They didn't go to this much effort to escape the first time to just give in now. Chey silently moved down the staircase and into the pitch-dark cellar. It wasn't big enough to be called a basement. Chey curled her lip at the pungent scent of damp rotting earth that stung her nostrils and made her eyes water. This place desperately needed an airing out.

She jumped when someone touched her shoulder. A hand whipped up and covered her mouth, and in a whirl of dust, she swung around to come face to face with Malcolm. The scream she'd been ready to let loose died on her tongue. He'd managed to close the cellar door and get down the stairs behind her without so much as a single creak. His ability to move astounded her.

He motioned her to remain quiet before slowly releasing the death grip across her face. She had so many questions about what the hell they were doing down here it nearly killed her to keep them inside. Even the slightest sound could alert whoever was in the house to their whereabouts. And they were definitely in the house.

There'd been a single creak above their heads only seconds ago. Chey glanced around the room searching for something—hell anything that gave her a sign of his plan. Except there was nothing here. Four walls, stinky dirty and stairs leading back into the house and in the hands of their would-be captors.

After what felt like hours but was probably only about forty-five minutes, Malcolm pulled her close and whispered again at her ear, "I think it's safe to move but we still have to be careful and not make a sound. They haven't gone far."

"You really think they're still here?" she mouthed.

"Ben is a patient hunter. More so than anyone I've ever met. He's waiting somewhere close by."

Chey nodded. Emotion knotted her stomach. Not exactly fear. Okay, maybe a little fear. Getting dragged in front of the cougar council by Ben and that bitch wasn't exactly her idea of a good time. Humiliation was definitely not her thing. Finding the bastard who killed John — now that's all that mattered.

"How do you propose we get out of the house?"

Malcolm flashed his teeth in a wicked grin that looked more like a snarl to her. "Ye of little faith. No hidey hole is worth dick if there isn't more than one way out." His head inclined toward the far corner and she zeroed in on the location searching for a door. Still nothing. He silently laughed and Chey bit back an angry retort. Now he was just playing with her.

Malcolm gripped her hand and pulled her to the far edge of the tiny room. His head whipped around and his eyes glowed gold. "What?" she mouthed again.

He didn't answer her right away instead his head turned to the left and right while he scanned the space above their heads. She heard nothing. Apparently satisfied that it was clear, Malcolm reached into the darkness and a small square door opened and a faint light filtered through the room. He pushed her through the space and quickly stepped through himself, only stopping to close the hatch behind them. He took the lead and Chey stayed on his tail. No point in getting separated now.

They were in a small underground tunnel that forced her to stoop as she walked. The smell seemed even worse in here with rotting vegetation lining the walls. When this was all over, she'd need an hour-long soak and some bath salts from hell to wash this stench away. About forty yards from where they'd exited the tunnel ended. The exit was covered by thick brush covered in brambles but she could see plenty of daylight on the other side, as well as hear the faint sounds of water. A stream probably.

Malcolm reached in front of her and ripped a hole through all of the debris. Her lips curled into a slight smile as she watched his naked ass. With every new flex of muscle she grew turned on. Soon he'd notice and then where the hell would they be? Suddenly, despite her usual comfort with being nude she was getting damn sick and tired of being naked.

"You need to shift before you go through the hole. There is a modicum of cover on this part of the property but it's not going to do much good if Ben is watching. We're going to have to make a run for it."

"Why the hell didn't you say something about this little exit sooner? What was the point of waiting and risking being caught?" Chey grabbed onto the annoyance and let it build. Better anger than arousal.

"Because that's exactly what they were expecting and I'd bet Ben had the perimeter covered."

"So if that's the case why go now?"

"Don't you feel the tension around the house? Enough time has passed that they are starting to believe we got away. They're restless and ready to leave."

Chey had her doubts about his reasoning but her own animal was getting edgy. She didn't want to stay still any longer. Better to make a run for it and let the chips fall. They had the advantage of Malcolm knowing the area. "Are you going to be able to—"

"Shift? Yeah. It'll probably still hurt like a bitch but it will get easier."

"Then you go first."

Malcolm shrugged and the air shimmered around him. Bones popped and muscles stretched but there were no cries of agony this time. Either he'd found a way to suck it up or he'd been right and this time was easier. In seconds, the heavy head of the black cougar turned and stared at her. His golden gaze settled on her, making her body heat against her will. Would there ever come a time when she didn't respond to him? She doubted it. From the first moment she'd laid eyes on him, she'd been lost. His strength mesmerized her and his scent called out to her, but it was always the raw dark emotion that she saw in his eyes that made it impossible for her to turn away. She didn't understand it, doubted she ever would. Still it haunted her.

Chey blinked her eyes against the past memories and focused on the now. She called for her cougar. She'd need the extra speed to escape. Escape. What a joke. Where exactly would she escape? Malcolm seemed hell bent on keeping her...at least until she told him the truth. Then what? It would always be Malcolm she ached for, no matter how hurt or angry he made her. A hard shudder worked up her spine as the change took over and she fell down on her hands. She lifted her head and once again met the golden gaze of her mate. As soon as they got clear, she'd have to sit him down and define what she thought of being a mate for him. There were just some things he needed to get out of his head, and the sooner the better.

To her surprise, he nuzzled against her fur. A low purr rumbled through her. What the hell? A fucking purr. Chey took two steps away from Malcolm and hissed in warning. They didn't have time for this. He looked at her with what she would have sworn was a mocking grin before turning and leaping through the exit. Chey followed suit and wanted to cry when the fresh air hit her face. *Yes!*

Malcolm moved in a blur and Chey took off at a dead run to keep up. She followed him, the freedom of a run taking over everything else. The warm breeze across her fur caught her by surprise when she sailed over the many fallen branches. For a second, she'd almost forgotten the danger they were in until she heard the sound of voices drifting through the leaves. Her muscles jerked and her head turned in the direction of the talking. For a split second she lost her concentration and she landed on a branch far too small to hold her weight. The resulting crack of it breaking underneath her might as well have been a loud signal flare saying "here we are."

She froze, afraid to move and give away her position until a low growl sounded ahead of her. Malcolm. She met his gaze and somehow she read his meaning. He wanted her to run. Her heart pounded frantically in her chest while she debated for a few seconds more. The voices she'd heard had ceased and the forest had gone deathly still. There were too many damn predators in this area. The smaller wildlife didn't love that any more than she did. The whole situation with Malcolm made her question everything. He wanted her trust. He asked for too much.

CHAPTER
THIRTEEN

Malcolm sensed the instant her mind had given into the fear. She was one of the strongest women he'd ever met, but her inability to trust belonged on his shoulders. They didn't have time for her to think about the right decision so he ran back to her position and nipped at her neck—a little harder than she'd like.

She hissed and snarled but at least he had her attention. He bit again. This time she got the message and took off running in basically the direction he'd been going. Despite the sound of his heavy breathing, the eerie calm in the air unnerved him. Every instinct in his body screamed in warning. Ben was close. Too close.

Dammit, Chey!

A gunshot tore through the trees without warning. Malcolm ran harder but it was too late. Pain crashed through his hip, a flash of heat searing through his legs and back. He fought the overload of sensation and attempted to power his hind legs harder. Fresh agony ripped through his insides, frying his brain and nearly taking him down. From a deep well of reserves he'd not accessed in a very long time, he pulled the energy to keep going. *Mate. Have to protect her.*

He cursed Ben and Chey both. One of these days, hopefully sooner rather than later, he'd turn that bastard into the hunted and see how he liked it. Shooting in the direction of a cougar's mate was more than enough reason to get you killed. He listened for pursuit and heard nothing beyond the blood rushing in his ears. *Fuck.*

Malcolm kept running. For how long he had no idea. It took every ounce of concentration he could muster just to put one foot in front of another while trying to keep pace with Chey. She moved fast too. He'd intended to lead his mate to safety but she'd surprised him with her knowledge of the area. So far she'd not taken a single misstep. Until now. She veered off toward the mountain instead of the deep forest that would take them to clan land. Exhaustion had begun to set in and he couldn't last much longer.

He tried to growl but it came out more like a croak. He had to get her attention. Malcolm stopped, took a deep breath and forced out the pain and weariness and focused on his mate. He couldn't leave her unprotected. He needed to shift and see about getting the bullet out of his hip so he could heal. The familiar power skated up his spine and the change swept over him hard and fast despite his injury. It was amazing what a body could take when it came to the need to protect. He gathered his voice and yelled as loud as he could, then fell over, his lungs laboring for breath.

She came back for him as the woman. "Malcolm, what the hell? Is this what you've become away from the— oh my god! What happened? Is that a—You've been shot."

"Yeah," he groaned.

"And you've been running for hours? What the hell is wrong with you?"

"We weren't safe. Had to get away."

She knelt down beside his hip and touched his burning flesh. "I can't believe they shot you. I swear when this is over I'm going to kill him myself."

Malcolm forced himself not to grin. Pain be damned. It was well worth it to see the concern etched on her face. "Get in line," he grumbled.

"We've got to get the bullet out so you can shift again. Dammit. We should have done this hours ago. Good thing you're already hurt or I might've kicked your ass."

"Nice to know you think so highly of me." He winced when her fingers pressed down on the edges of the open wound.

"I'm going to need something to get this out." She stood and turned away, surveying the area.

"I think you should—"

"Just shut up. I'm really pissed off right now and I need to think."

Malcolm clamped his jaw shut and stopped talking. He didn't feel like arguing at the moment. Spots swam in his vision and nausea curled in his stomach. He'd lost a lot of blood on the run and he needed to shift again soon. To take his mind off the throbbing pain, his brain tuned into the rhythm of the forest around them. Wind wandered through the trees, rustling the leaves. Small wildlife, sensing no danger, went about their business despite the scent of his sweat and blood tainting the area.

"We might not have much time. I probably left a damn easy trail for Ben to follow."

"Good. Then I can kick his ass when he shows up. I'm going to need more than a dirty stick to help you. I need a damned knife." She brushed away the hair from his eyes and mopped the sweat from his brow. He wondered if she even realized how intimate the move actually was. "Lucky for you, I have my own hidey holes and that's exactly where we were headed."

"You have a hideout on the edge of clan property?" Was she crazy too? If he'd caught her kind stalking the area, the first thing he'd have done was eliminate the threat or at the very least report her to the council. They didn't take that shit lightly.

"Surprising isn't it? What can I say? I like to live dangerously."

"Death wish maybe."

"Stop whining and lie still. Your pale skin and cold sweat is starting to worry me."

"It's going to take a lot more than a bullet hole to take me down, sweetheart."

She rolled her eyes and shifted. The change took her so fast he barely saw it. Pale fur filled his vision. Unable to resist touching her, he stroked her pelt, luxuriating in the silky softness of her coat. He knew she still harbored a lot of reservations about him and he didn't blame her. Not that it would stop him from keeping her. Her amber gaze met his and he recognized the hesitation immediately. He allowed his hand to fall free from her fur, but his eyes tracked her as long as he could until she disappeared from sight.

For a few seconds, he considered dragging his sorry ass into the brush in an attempt to stay hidden and decided against it. Why bother? If someone like Ben or any other shifter tracked him, no flimsy bush would hide his bloody carcass. He laid back and thought about why Chey needed a hiding spot so close to clan land. He'd purposely not sought any information on her after he'd walked away. In his mind, a clean break for them both was the best option he could give her. She could move on and he would live up to his family duty. Of course, that plan had gone to shit within a matter of months. The look on her face when he'd left her behind still haunted him.

"WHY ARE YOU DOING THIS?" Tears tracked down her face, each one sending a dagger straight through his heart.

"This was a mistake from the beginning. If I'd known you were a hybrid this never would have happened." He turned away from the look of horror on her face. "We do not mix with wolves. It's forbidden and you damn well know it."

A choked sob sounded behind him, sending his cat into a tizzy. The scent of her sex still drove them both crazy and it took a herculean amount of effort to not turn back.

"Go home, Cheyenne. Back to your own kind. I don't want to see you on clan land again. You're definitely not welcome here and I won't be held responsible if you cross the line again."

HIS ENTIRE BODY had ached to turn back. To gather her in his arms and make any kind of promise that would bind her to him. But after losing his father so close after his mother's suicide, he had a duty he owed to his brothers. At the time, he'd had no idea what turning his back on a true bond mate would do to his frame of mind. That it would chip away at his sanity one cold fraction at a time.

What had happened to her? Malcolm opened his eyes and struggled to focus. His vision wouldn't focus no matter how hard he tried. The waning light gave way to darkness in the blink of an eye. His mouth was so dry it ached, making it almost impossible to swallow, and now his limbs shook. Annoyed with his weakness, Malcolm dragged himself to a sitting position. Pain shot through his body from hip to ankle.

"What the hell are you doing? I told you I'd be right back." He sagged in relief at the sexy sound of her voice.

"You've been gone so long I thought maybe Ben had tracked you instead of me."

She knelt next to him. "I was only gone thirty minutes. You must be really out of it. Here, I brought you this." She held up a bottle of water.

"Thanks," he muttered but made no move to take the bottle.

Chey brushed the hair out of his eyes. "You're a mess." She unscrewed the top of the water and brought the plastic to his lips. Cool water splashed over his tongue and soothed his desert dry throat. "I'm going to get that bullet out now so you can shift and we can get the hell out of here. First, lie back down."

Her voice was gentle, soothing even. Too bad it took getting shot to see her like this. She'd make an incredible mother someday. Malcolm groaned. The combination of pain flaring in his hip and the image of her pregnant with his child did him in. Not once had he allowed himself to believe in a family of his own. Bastards like him weren't father material.

"You sure are bossy," he said.

She ignored him and he nearly whimpered at the first brush of her fingers across his skin. A shock of need fired through his blood. Half out of his mind from blood loss and still all he thought about was how incredible it felt to be inside her. All that wet heat tightening around him. He groaned again.

"Quit being such a baby. You'll be fine in about ten minutes."

Maybe his hip would be. The rest of him raged for the woman kneeling by his side. "You shouldn't be here. Kane had no business bringing you into all of this."

She snorted. "You don't know the half of it. But you will."

Before he could question what she meant, a sharp bladed knife pushed through his bullet hole. Flames licked at his skin and he had to grind his jaw together to keep quiet. His vision went dark with a violent urge to fight back ripping through his skin. The second she got the bullet dislodged the change overtook him. Again, fast and wickedly painful. Bones snapped and twisted. Someone might as well have stuck a hot flaming poker into his wound. He roared long and loud. Rage fueled him.

Every painful moment of the last few years flew through his memory. He'd tried to do the right thing and failed. He'd left his brothers to save them from what he was turning into and someone had taken advantage of them all. Now he was going to find the bastard and bring him down. Pain gave way to power, healing him from the inside out.

His vision cleared and with it a complete awareness of everything around him. Home. Chey had led him to within a few miles from Kane's cabin. The time for running away from their problems had ended. They'd make a stand now or die trying. Too much bullshit kept happening at the hands of a council hiding behind a bunch of antiquated laws.

He opened his mouth and another roar burst from him.

"I take it you're feeling better now."

Malcolm's head jerked in her direction. Despite the blood on her hands she looked more beautiful than ever. She'd obviously had clothes hidden away along with her knife. Although the denim shorts and tank top she'd donned did nothing to cover her long bare limbs. The memory of her sexy skin slicked with sweat and sliding across his body caught him off guard. She'd scraped her long blonde hair into a ponytail at the base of her head, which did nothing at all to detract from her sexual allure. Even the sweat trickling along the edge of her face called to him on the most primal level. He closed his eyes and breathed deep, letting her scent fill his senses.

He growled at her.

She stepped toward him, her hand extended. If she touched him, he'd be lost. And as much as he wanted to get far inside her right now, it was not the right time. For all he knew, Ben had circled around and was coming for them from the inside. Until they got to Kane's place and demanded some answers, she wasn't safe. And if there was one thing that would never be up for debate it'd be his need to keep his mate safe.

He whirled away from her and launched through the brush. His ears perked up waiting for a tell tale sign she followed. When he finally heard her less than graceful stomping through the bushes and a few muttered curses under her breath, he smiled and bounded toward home. They would settle this once and for all.

AFTER A FEW GLORIOUS miles of running through his childhood memories in the form of his favorite part of the forest, Malcolm shifted and emerged from the trees. Kane stood in front of his cabin waiting, with his new mate Lara not far behind.

"Look what the cat dragged—" Lara stopped before she finished. She probably realized what an asinine statement that made now that she'd discovered her shifter heritage.

"And how is that shifting coming these days, my sweet?" Malcolm drawled.

Chey growled behind him. The sound low and vicious.

"Easy now. I'm not in the mood for breaking up another catfight. I only recently got all the blood out of the carpet from the last time." Kane walked into the clearing and pulled Lara to his side. Malcolm wasn't sure when he'd get used to seeing them together. He'd used her mercilessly in his attempt to strike back at the clan for making him an outcast, and she'd been all too willing to go along with him. Not like he was one to cast stones. He shook his head. The pain of not shifting had been unbearable after the first year. The only way he'd managed to get through each day had been to execute his pent up rage in one scheme after another. Gods, his brothers should have killed him by now.

Malcolm tucked Chey into his side before facing his brother. "What's going on with Lucas? Have you convinced him to return yet?"

"I think he and Kira will show. But it's not going to be easy to convince the council to let them stay. They fear the psy clan even more than the wolves."

"I don't really care. This is our land, our clan. We have as much right as anyone else, possibly more so."

"That kind of attitude isn't going to get you very far," Kane responded. "We need to tread carefully."

"Since when do I play nice or do politics well? Someone on that council is seriously fucking with us and it's time to find out who."

The room grew uncomfortably silent and everyone avoided looking at him. Even Chey tensed against his side. The tension stifled the air and he immediately sensed a revelation that was about to piss him off. Royally.

"Godsdamnit. What?" He eyed each one of them warily. They met him with complete silence and little eye contact. He grabbed Chey by the shoulders and forced her to look at him. "Tell me."

"You might as well. He's got the scent now and no amount of avoidance will save any of us at this point."

Malcolm swung his gaze at his brother and lowered his voice. "Someone had better start talking and right now. I don't enjoy being the only one out of the loop."

After several more long, tense seconds, Chey spoke up. "Kane already knows who it is."

Malcolm took a step back. "What?" An immediate swell of resentment buzzed in his head.

"I've suspected for a while now and when Chey approached me with some pretty compelling evidence, I put two and two together and that's when I decided it was time to pull you back in. I don't disagree with you about the council. Their effectiveness has diminished and it's time to take our clan back."

"Wait. You've known all along? Why didn't you tell me?" He stared down Chey, forgetting that Lara and Kane stood nearby. The old familiar distrust rushing forward. *Never trust a wolf.* How many times had that fact been drilled into his head? His lip curled into a snarl before he could stop it.

"I wasn't one hundred percent certain."

"Who is it?"

"I needed your help to be sure. Besides, you had to figure this out for yourself. Force feeding you the truth wouldn't get you to accept it."

"Tell me who."

"You know who," she cried. Chey backed up a few steps. She must have recognized the rage.

"Calm down, Malcolm. Getting pissed at Chey isn't going to help this mess at all. Let her finish."

Malcolm clenched his jaw and stared into the violent storm brewing in her eyes. The lead weight in his stomach didn't bode well for his sanity. "Who?" he demanded.

"Bran." Her voice trembled.

"Our uncle? Why?" He didn't want to believe it, but she'd been right. He'd had his own suspicions.

Chey shrugged. "I don't know for sure. I figured you might have the answer to that better than I."

"He's crazy, Mal. Always has been. I'm sure you remember the vicious fights between him and Dad. I thought with him gone, our illustrious uncle might get over his insane jealousy but I guess I was wrong."

He shook his head. "That makes no sense. And what the hell does that have to do with you?" He pointed his finger at Chey. She was holding something more back still. His gut screamed with it.

"He's the one who killed John. I'd been hunting the killer for a while before I realized who he might be. For months, it drove me crazy why his scent was so damned familiar. But it wasn't until… "

Malcolm's head filled with images of another man touching Chey. Rage fed the crazy he barely managed to control. He growled.

Chey rolled her eyes. "You are seriously going to have to get past this. His name is going to come up." She approached him. "You walked away. Do I really have to keep reminding you?" Her finger poked him in the chest. "I moved on. Life fucking happens."

"Easy, Chey." Kane's warning to his mate only angered him further.

"Stay out of it, brother." He grabbed Chey's wrist and twisted it behind her back. Her eyes turned molten. She was certainly annoyed but it didn't dampen the desire he sensed from her. "I thought I was doing the right thing. I certainly didn't know I was about to ruin my entire life."

Chey stiffened against him a millisecond before she sprung. She twisted free from his hold and smashed her leg into his gut, sending him flying into the dirt. Before his head even bounced from the ground she grabbed his arms and pinned him down. "Do you ever think of anyone other than yourself?" She bared her teeth and growled. Not the cat—the wolf. "You aren't the only one who's suffered over the years."

Malcolm grabbed her around the waist. "I've thought of—"

"Mommy are you okay?"

Both their heads swung in the direction of the young voice. Chey moved so fast Malcolm barely saw it. She'd released him and scooped up the child in the blink of an eye.

"Allie baby, mommy's fine. How did you get here? Where's nana?"

Mommy?

Malcolm's head buzzed with the implication. No wonder she was so determined to avenge her dead husband. She had a child. All the air leeched from his body and his blood ran cold. Another man fathered a child with his mate. Good thing John was already dead or he'd have to kill him. Already his instincts sought retribution.

"The pretty lady brought me here."

"What? What lady?"

"She showed up on our doorstep right before you did. Someone rang the bell and left her there. Don't worry, we checked her over and she seems unhurt. She took to Lara immediately, and after breakfast she fell asleep in the guest room."

Malcolm stared at the child looking over Chey's shoulder, barely comprehending a word Kane said. Silky black curls framed a beautiful face with wide-set deep green eyes. She was the complete opposite of her mother and instead bore a remarkable resemblance to... Two tiny tears rolled from her eyes, interrupting his thoughts, and the scent of fear permeated the area. As if drawn by a magnetic pull, Malcolm crossed the clearing and approached the child. Her beauty mesmerized him in a way that only one other female ever had. The babe's mother.

He reached for her and she innocently lifted her arms to him as well.

"Malcolm, what are you..."

The scent of the child drifted over him as she settled in his arms. A beautiful blend of her mother and wild nature, her small heart beating against his chest. Malcolm held her close and inhaled deeply. His cougar acknowledged her instinctively and yowled for a second before it settled into a slow purr. *Oh dear goddess. Not another man's child. His child.*

"How old are you, sweetheart?"

"I'm this many." She smiled and held up four fingers.

The pit in his stomach sank and a new anger rushed through his blood. He fought the urge to turn on the girl's mother. But he'd lost so much time.

"Malcolm we need to talk—"

"No." His firm statement startled the girl, she whimpered and fear once again crossed her face.

"It's okay, sweetheart. You're safe with me. Always safe." He patted her back and turned away from prying eyes as he fought his own tears. He had a child. It was far more than a man like him deserved. "What's your name?"

"Allie," she whispered. The smell of fear had not completely dissipated.

His brain wanted to be angry, to rage at the woman who'd hidden his child, but his damn instincts wouldn't allow it. He had to protect the babe at all costs. Still, he couldn't look at Chey. He didn't want to know what emotions played across her face at the sight of her child—their child in his arms.

"Malcolm, we need to talk about this. She's not safe here."

His lip curled and a growl escaped before he could stop it. He whirled on Chey. "You think I can't protect my own child? If Bran so much as comes near her, I'll rip his throat out myself."

Chey's eyes narrowed and her lips pursed together. "He killed John trying to find her. I hid her well after that and no way could he have gotten to her unless..."

"Unless what?"

"Unless my mother is dead."

Allie started crying in his arms. Chey stepped toward him and his cougar growled in warning.

"Dammit, Malcolm. We don't have time for this. Allie is scared and you're only making it worse."

"You can't have her." Uncontrollable rage washed over him. He glanced at everyone in the clearing, watching each and every one of them stare at him in fear. "Give me a break. What do you expect? I learned I have a four-year-old babe and the minute I scented her, a bond began to form. Now you think I'll just hand her over to the woman who didn't want me to know about her?"

Kane stepped forward. "Be reasonable, Malcolm. Ever since you walked away from her you've been a different man."

"A scary one most of the time," Lara piped up.

Malcolm snarled.

"Malcolm, please. I understand how you feel. When I found John lying in a pool of warm blood with my knife stuck in his chest, I freaked out. Then he told me that the killer knew who Allie was and I nearly went crazy with rage. Every instinct screamed to go after him. If it wasn't for her I don't know what would have happened. Somehow her presence made me realize that my revenge had to be smart. That I couldn't take too many chances with my life when I had someone counting on me to be there. For months, I searched and sought a way to get to him. When the trail grew cold and I knew I had to get on clan land, I came to Kane. To you. The man I knew would hate me once he learned the truth."

Malcolm soaked in the pain of her words. The love she clearly felt for a dead man. Anger, sadness, fear, rage— she had it all in spades. He knew the feeling well. He'd fucked up everything on that fateful day. Goddess never in his wildest dreams had he once even considered she'd be with child. Pain lashed through his gut. Regret. Sorrow.

"I had to leave. My obligation was to my brother and clan." The old excuse sounded hollow to his ears now.

Kane stepped forward. "Nothing should ever come before a man and his mate, brother. Nothing. I would have gladly told you that if you'd come to me or Lucas. You see what happened to us when our fate came calling. You can't change fate, especially now. That beautiful babe is all that matters. Forget the past and think of your future. Dammit man, you have always been your own worst enemy. Do you think we could get past that now?"

"Easy for you to say." He could barely think straight let alone be reasonable. His mate didn't love a dead man.

Allie cried harder and nothing he whispered in her ear or touch he offered consoled her. She wanted her mother. Reluctantly, Malcolm handed her to Chey. For a split second, pain threatened to tear his skull in two when he relinquished his daughter. A primal urge far deeper than he'd accessed before wouldn't let her go. His arms and legs shook from the force of it.

Lara stepped in Chey's path. "Let me take her so you and Malcolm can have this out."

"No!" Malcolm raged.

"Yes." Kane stepped closer and placed himself between Malcolm and Chey. "I'm still the guardian here and the current family leader. My mate will take good care of her."

"But—"

"Shut up, Mal and talk to your mate. She needs you too, you know."

Malcolm snorted at that. What a joke.

Lara removed Allie from Chey's embrace and he fought the urge to take her back and wrap his hands around the witch's neck until she stopped breathing. Half shifter or not, he hadn't adjusted to her place in their family one bit.

"Don't even think about it. You might be my brother but I *will* kill you if you make a move against my mate," Kane warned.

Common sense warred with the insane need to protect his child. In his heart, he knew Kane had nothing but the best intentions, and if he trusted his mate then she would be a trustworthy caregiver. If only the crazy train of his brain would listen and let go. Before his mother and father's death, there had been no real anger between the brothers. They'd laughed and played and fought side by side every single day. Had five years really passed since their lives had all changed?

"Isn't this sweet?"

They all jerked to face the direction of the sickly sweet voice. Kitty, Bran's only child, stood behind them. Her eyes glittered with a sick anger and an even sicker sneer plastered across her lips.

"Lara, run!" Kane ordered.

"No. I haven't come here to harm anyone as much as I might like to." She snarled in Lara's direction.

"If you do, you'll die where you stand." Kane looked ready to spring. "Haven't we all suffered through enough of your petty jealousy?"

Kitty shrugged. "Threatening me isn't going to get you much. But you might want to hear what I have to say before you act too rashly."

"I doubt you have anything to say that we'd be interested in. Unless of course you'd like to tell us where your father is." Malcolm stalked closer to Kitty, making sure to block her view from Lara and his child.

A wide smile spread across her face. "Finally starting to wise up to what's going on under your own noses, are you? I thought you'd never catch on."

Malcolm gritted his teeth against the need to teach the female feline a lesson in the form of a serious ass kicking. Kitty caused nothing but trouble at every opportunity and he trusted her even less now in the face of the facts against Bran.

"Where is the bastard?"

She leaned against the tree she'd emerged from behind. "You mean dear old dad?" She shrugged. "I guess you haven't heard then that the council convened this morning. Looks like you two are missing your own trial." She motioned to him and Chey.

"Oh for cripes sake. Would you get to the point already? I'm getting bored over here." He didn't care about anything but finding Bran. And if the council was having a session then it was the perfect time to interrupt. "Let's go. We don't have time for her." He motioned to Kane.

"Hold on there, Mr. Big Bad Ass Black Cougar. If you go running in there without any evidence against my father you'll end up executed before nightfall."

Malcolm snorted. "You're assuming they have someone who can handle us."

Kitty sighed. "Your arrogance is going to get you no where. Do you honestly think they haven't prepared for this? Fine. Go ahead. When you're both dead I'll enjoy telling your mates I told you so."

Kane stepped forward. "Kitty what do you want? Seriously."

"Let's just say I'm sick of the bullshit. Do you have any idea what it's like to be under his thumb every day? Lately I've been afraid to even sleep in the same house.

I have no friends, no family to turn to. Hell, I have no life. It's always been about you and you." She pointed to Kane and then Malcolm.

"I'm not buying it. You've delivered some low blows yourself." Kitty had always been just as conniving as her father. She'd managed to seduce her way through his brothers and when neither would take her as a mate she'd gone off the deep end and attacked Lara.

"Fuck you, Malcolm. You haven't exactly been lily white these past few years. At least I haven't tried to kill anyone."

"Yet." Kane added.

"Why are we listening to her?" Lara asked.

"Because I have information you might want, sweetheart," Kitty drawled.

"I'll show you sweetheart in a minute."

"Enough." Kane boomed. "We don't have time for this. Either tell us something useful or get the fuck off my land."

"That's just it." Kitty pulled a piece of paper out of her back pocket and unfolded it. The worn copy looked about ready to fall apart. "If you want me off your property then I'd have to leave the clan." She handed the paper over to Kane and took a step back when Lara growled at her. "Look, I realize it's a day late and a dollar short but I came to do the right thing before I leave."

Malcolm glanced over his brother's shoulder and read the paper along with him. If it was to be believed, his family did own clan land. Along with guardianship came ownership. "You think this has something to do with the crap Bran has been pulling?"

She shrugged. "I think it did at one time but my father is gone now."

"What do you mean gone? Where the hell did he go?"

"Not that kind of gone. He's gone crazy. Loco. Insane. The minute she showed up he freaked and hasn't been the same." Kitty pointed at Lara.

"Me? What, because of Nick?" Malcolm had heard all about the death of Kane's childhood friend at the hands of a half-shifted Lara. Nick had attacked her and in the moment of trying to escape her adrenalin had spiked and her shifter side had strained for dominance. Something he nor Kane would have expected for nothing.

Kitty roared with laughter. A mocking sound that grated on his nerves. "Fools all of you. I can't believe I have to tell you this." She narrowed her eyes and focused on Lara. "Who do you think it is who fathered you? The shifter fairy?"

Silence descended among the group until Allie's whimpering broke the quiet. Lara's face had turned ghostly white and the child had sensed her distress.

"He wants her too. He thinks the baby is an abomination. I wasn't exaggerating when I said crazy. Just be glad she wasn't a boy. If he'd thought for a second your baby was born a black cougar he'd have stopped at nothing until it died."

Chey stepped forward. "This is all too ridiculous. Why? What did he have to gain from all of this?"

"I don't think it had anything to do with gaining and instead had everything to do with—"

"I think that's quite enough Kitty, don't you?" said a new voice.

CHAPTER
FOURTEEN

Bran emerged from a clump of trees to their side. How the hell he'd gotten so close without his scent giving him away Malcolm couldn't fathom. He looked every inch the perfect councilman dressed impeccably in his freshly pressed slacks and button down white shirt. Except for two things. The wild, unfocused look in his eyes and the black pistol he held in his hand.

"Didn't know you were followed, huh? I knew you were always worth nothing. I should have put you down long ago." Before anyone could respond, Bran shot Kitty in the stomach. The sound tore through the area, quickly followed by Allie's shrieks.

"Shut the baby up before I do." Bran commanded. He leveled his gun in Allie's direction and Malcolm's cougar took over. Claws ripped through his skin, fur bristled across his arms mere seconds before he prepared to jump on his uncle. "Move and I shoot. Do you think you can shift and pounce faster than a bullet?"

Malcolm's blood froze. The cougar screamed in his head but the logic of the man won out. He clamped on his control as he glanced around their rag tag group: Kitty bleeding on the ground with no one able to get near her, Lara holding his child with Chey standing guard in front of them, and Kane by his side waiting for the right moment to jump Bran.

The pungent scent coming from his uncle clogged his senses and turned his stomach. It wasn't exactly fear but it wasn't confidence either. More like righteous indignation. Kitty was right. He was plain nuts. The urge to eliminate the threat clawed through the beast inside him. It took every ounce of control he had to hold onto the human half of him. His bond with Chey had gone a long way to correcting the imbalance between man and animal but it wasn't enough. His experiences had shaped him into a different man—a harsher one that could no longer conform to the rules he'd sworn to live by as a cub.

The hate he'd allowed to seep into his life had become a part of him and he doubted even Chey could eliminate it.

Allie cried harder, reaching for her mother.

Bran pointed the gun at Chey's head. "Touch her and you both die."

Chey hesitated and Malcolm calculated the distance between him and his uncle and exactly how long it would take to block him. Damn bastard. "Guns are for cowards." He couldn't help taunting the asshole.

"Guns will keep your ass in line. And your half-breed too."

"You aren't getting out of here alive, uncle. So what is it you want?"

"If any of you kill a council member without sanction you'll all be executed." He shifted his stance. "Don't you get it? I've done everything I've done for the good of the clan and everyone knows it. I'm the only one of those bastards who was really willing to get his hands dirty when they grew tired of your father's power. They wanted someone who would toe the line and he wasn't it. It was supposed to be me. I was born first. The dominant gene is always carried through the first-born child. Always."

"You're going to die a lonely old man with nothing at all because you've let jealousy eat you alive. No one controls Mother Nature and even you know that," Kane said, his voice rumbling.

"You are so stupid. The luck of your DNA may have made you Guardian, but for the last five years you've done as I directed. At least until you brought her here." Bran sneered at Lara. "You were the worst mistake of my life. If only Nick had done as he was supposed to.

"What?" Malcolm and Kane yelled in unison.

"Her bitch of a mother promised me a child of my own making, but all I got was yet another bastard whore like that one." Bran swung his gun wildly toward Kitty. "Hell, I even thought just maybe Malcolm's half-breed mate might produce an heir I could claim as my own. Imagine my surprise when her useless substitute mate revealed the child was a girl while blood gurgled in his throat. At least he'd tried to protect them. Unlike you."

Hot blood red rage filled Malcolm's vision. In the back of his mind he heard someone shriek and all hell broke loose. The half wolf form of his mate sailed through the air, headed straight for Bran. Her bones and muscles popped and stretched the whole time until the wolf fully emerged. Bran, far more agile than Malcolm had expected, shot his gun and leapt toward her. The wolf cried out and fell, crumpled to the ground, blood spatter spraying Malcolm's shirt.

The scent of his mate in pain unleashed the beast he'd tried to control. A roar emerged from deep within, startling everyone around him. *Mate. Mine.* The familiar pain of his shift rushed over him, taking complete control of the human and shoving him aside. Until Allie screaming behind him caught his attention.

Her cries turned to pain filled wails and they all turned to focus on her. Oh holy hell. She was going through a change. The adrenalin from her fear must have brought it on.

"Allie!" Chey cried from the ground, her wolf form gone. "Let me help her. This is her first shift."

"No." Bran stepped on Chey's wound and the guttural cry of fresh pain filled the night air and shook him to his core. Bran might as well have been peeling the flesh from his bones. The man reemerged, fighting for breath and control.

The sound of the babe's bones snapping and her muscles tearing ripped through Malcolm's guts. Chey ignored Bran's warnings and locked her gaze on him.

Save my child, she mouthed.

Malcolm focused his gaze on his uncle and moved to block his child. "If you kill her, you die." He paused. "You know what? Fuck that. You're already a dead man."

"What the hell?" Bran's gaze locked on the girl behind him.

Malcolm turned to Lara and swallowed hard. Struggling in her arms he found the impossible. A fully shifted black cougar cub. He couldn't even fathom how that was possible. Never in centuries of history between Scotland and North America had there ever been a documented female black cougar.

Before Malcolm could move, the cub scrambled from Lara's arms and hit the ground feet first. She yowled at Bran and leapt in his direction.

"No!" Chey yelled at her daughter, fear stopping her heart. Oh Goddess, please. She struggled against Bran's hold until the pain blinded her. In her peripheral vision she watched helplessly as he raised his gun and aimed at her beautiful baby cougar trying to protect its mother.

Malcolm, partially shifted, leapt on a soul splitting roar. Chey would swear later her bones shook from the force of it. He blocked Allie's jump and landed on top of Bran. The gun went off again but Malcolm didn't stop. In the violent frenzy, Chey was able to hobble across the clearing and scoop up Allie. She'd already shifted back to the adorable child Chey'd done everything to protect and failed miserably at.

Tears tracked down Allie's face as she held her close. "It's okay, honey. Mama is here." But Allie knew it was not all right. How could she not with the wild shrieks behind her?

"Kane, do something to help him," she demanded.

He shook his head. "No, this is his fight now. You know damn well he'd probably tear my head off if I didn't let him do this."

"If he dies, then I'm going to strangle you. How's that?" The thought of Malcolm losing turned her blood cold and wrenched her gut. She couldn't live without him now. The thought shocked her into place.

"Let me take Allie and get her away from here."

Chey turned away from Lara. "No."

"Then you do it. Your child's safety has to come first dammit."

Lara was right of course. Nothing mattered more than Allie's life, not even Malcolm's. He'd want it that way as much as she did. Tears rolled from her eyes. "I can't leave him. I can't."

"Then give me the babe and trust me to keep her safe." Chey glanced down at Allie's face buried at her breast. Her body shook like a leaf, breaking her heart. The scent of fear came so strong from her it nearly debilitated Chey. It probably proved a distraction for Malcolm as well.

"I can't leave, baby. But you have to." She pressed her lips to the dusty black curls on her head. "Lara will keep you safe while I help your daddy."

Before she could change her mind, she pulled Allie free and handed her over to Lara, who wasted no time running away.

"If anything happens to Malcolm, Bran won't leave here alive," Kane reassured her.

"He's not leaving alive no matter what happens." She'd kill him herself if she had to. Fear and anger fueled her now and both would work in her favor as powerful motivators.

Twilight had descended on the area and soon it would be black as night. Not that it affected any of their vision. They saw as good in the dark as they did during the day. Both men were now giant cats, rolling through the grass. Blood covered Bran's lighter coat and she suspected Malcolm's dark fur disguised the same. Claws and teeth swiped at each other until Bran managed to get the upper hand and his jaw bit down on Malcolm's throat.

In a split second, the air grew thick and still as Bran held Malcolm pinned to the ground. In a bold, possibly stupid move, Malcolm half shifted back to human and caught Bran off guard. He twisted his body and tore his way into Bran's chest. Teeth tightened around Malcolm's neck and Chey screamed.

Malcolm jerked his arm and pulled Bran's heart free from the cavity of his chest. "Take that motherfucker."

Malcolm tossed Bran's now lifeless body as easily as a rag doll to the forest floor and rose to his full height. Half cat and half human, he stood covered in bloody gashes across his skin, his eyes so gold it nearly hurt to look at them. He still held Bran's heart in his hands and he looked every inch the savage she'd suspected he'd become. Her heart beat wildly.

"Fuck, man. You are still one scary dude."

"Go away," Malcolm snarled at his brother.

"As if it's that easy. You've made quite a mess that's going to take some time to clean up."

"Not now, Kane," Malcolm warned again.

Kane started to say something and must have thought better of it. He pushed his way past his brother and scooped to pick up Kitty who still lay bleeding on the ground. The thick red liquid oozed through the hand she pressed to her stomach. Her eyes grew round.

"Don't look at me like that, woman. You may annoy the hell out of me but you have answers I need so I'm not about to let you die tonight."

"I don't have to tell you shit," she spat.

Kane laughed, a wholly evil sound. "Oh but you will. I promise you that." He turned and strode toward the cabin, leaving them alone at the edge of the forest.

Malcolm looked at the heart still gripped in his hand and his lip curled in disgust. On a grunt, he threw it as far away as possible. Chey didn't know what to say. He stood before her tore up from a fight without a stitch of clothes on and a hard on from hell. He'd obviously enjoyed killing Bran, and if she examined her own feelings, she'd discover her primal satisfaction as well. He'd done what it took to save their child and that's all that mattered to her.

"Chey," he whispered.

She loved the sound of her name when it fell from his lips. It always swept over her like a sensual caress. She darted forward and he immediately raised his hands to stop her. Puzzled, she stood transfixed and waited. The air shimmered and the magic of the shift swirled around her. He fell to the forest floor and the sleek black cat emerged for a few brief seconds before he shifted again and stood proud on his feet.

The gashes from his skin were now simply red streaks of skin knitted back together and most of the blood had fallen away as well. His amazing ability to heal still astounded her. She could do the same although on a much smaller scale. It sped the healing process but it was far from instant. Injuries like his would take much longer to heal in her.

"Are you hurt?" he asked, moving close. He pressed his hand to the soft skin of her side, scorching her already burning skin.

"Not badly. The bullet missed its intended target and only grazed my hip. The shift helped."

Malcolm growled an instant before he moved. Before she could blink, she was backed into a tree and his body pressed to hers. "You scared the hell out of me."

Moisture pooled between her thighs at the gruff tone of his voice. The harsh intensity in his eyes bored clear to her soul and caused a mass of butterflies to take flight in her stomach.

"I panicked and was running on pure instinct. I couldn't stand idly by and do nothing." He'd saved her child. Saved her. Hell, she couldn't think straight with his scent wrapped around her. She wanted him so damn bad her pulse beat wildly for him. "Thank you," she whispered.

"Don't. Look at me. This is who I am now. I'm not nice or cuddly by any stretch of the imagination. I've developed the habit of hurting those around me. You should run."

"I can see just fine. And I certainly don't have much right to expect perfection." Chey's insides trembled as she waited for his reaction. He'd barely discovered he had a child before he had to defend her life. When the adrenalin fueling him came down, he'd want nothing to do with her. But if all she had left was this moment now, she'd take it. She couldn't not.

"I need you, Malcolm," she confessed, bowing her head in submission.

He growled. "You have no idea what you're asking for." He rubbed his naked body against hers, his thick erection branding the warm skin of her lower abdomen. "Every minute I'm around you I want to fuck you. I always want to be inside you," he growled.

Goddess, she loved the need she heard in his voice. If only she could find a way to hold onto that and get them over the past. Her fingers tightened on his biceps when his fingers flicked across her aching nipples. She traced an angry looking red mark on his chest and leaned forward to press her lips to the skin. The dusting of hair on his chest tickled her nose and the scent of victory and horny man filled her senses.

She held tight and lifted from the ground, wrapping her legs around his waist. He probed her entrance, nudging the wet heat and sensitive folds until he slowly began to fill her. She sucked in a breath and nipped his nipple with her teeth. His head tipped back and he roared, shaking the tree and ground beneath them.

"Mine."

His exclamation surprised her. Yes, they'd been mated but that didn't mean love and happy endings, especially not after what they'd been through. "Malcolm. Yes. Ohhh. Yes." Violent sensations tore through her with every new inch of cock he fed her until she wanted to kick and scream and claw his eyes out for more. Never in her life had she felt this wild, this out of control for sex.

One hand slid behind her back and protected her from the rough bark of the tree but the other... Oh Goddess, his claws. He raked them across first one breast and then the other, eliciting shards of pleasure so intense she threatened to blow.

Her muscles clenched, clasping at his dick, sucking him deeper than before. "Oh yes, just like that."

"You're so demanding." He shoved to the hilt and the words she'd been about to say disappeared in a harsh exhalation of what little air she maintained in her lungs.

For a split second, she felt his warm breath across her cheek, a sensual brush of erotic hunger that pushed her to the edge of a frenzy before his lips captured hers. His tongue pushed between her lips and the familiar roughness started a firestorm inside of her. She moaned into him. And still with the damn claws! He dragged them across her skin with a firm stroke to the point of a strong sting that awakened every nerve ending he touched.

He sucked on her tongue and the last of her restraint melted under the onslaught. The kiss deepened as he withdrew to the tip. She whimpered into his mouth and dug into his skin to keep him from pulling out. His kisses were better than anything she'd ever imagined and she'd had some serious dreams about this man. He brushed his hands down her sides and around her thighs until his claw-tipped fingers brushed the soft skin of her nether lips that were stretched wide to accommodate him.

Malcolm licked and stroked her mouth while shuttling in and out of her excruciatingly slow. The pace maddened her but the second she moved to protest, his claws pricked her skin, stopping her movement. The scent of hot desire fueled by the excess adrenalin of the fight made her want to resist. She wanted to struggle. Chey clenched around his shaft with every ounce of strength she possessed until he broke the kiss and growled at her.

Despite the hard look in his eyes, the passion and need shone through. Malcolm thrust harder and Chey sensed the danger swirling around him. This man would always demand her submission—she felt it clear to her core. His features contorted and melded, making it apparent the beast resided side by side with the man.

Yet he gave her more than he ever took. Pleasure and protection. He'd been willing to lay down his life for not only their child—but her. Chey trembled with the fact. Her head tipped back. It was just the mate bond. It had to be. He hated her wolf.

He pumped harder, fucking her with a demand that pushed her ever closer to the edge. Oh Goddess, it was too much. She arched, angling for him to go deeper.

Once again, he growled at her in warning and she froze. He flashed his fangs. Her body quivered. Each stroke was hotter than the last, sending an agonizing flash of electricity across sensitive nerves. Only enough to keep her close and wanting just a little bit more. Dammit he wanted her to beg. And she wanted to. Goddess did she ever.

"Malcolm, please," she whimpered each time he bumped her needy bundle of nerves. "Please. Goddess. More."

Another growl, this time rumbling through his chest and belly and vibrating between her thighs. Sweat glistened on his skin, muscles strained for obvious control and the sweet musk of sex tormenting her. He leaned his body closer, creating more friction than ever as he hammered into her. She couldn't hold on. Chey locked her heels across his buttocks and screamed his name as a sudden wave of pleasure washed over her. She shook and shuddered in his arms as the onslaught continued one pulse after another. The explosions of color blinded her, and the world around her absorbed her screams of both pleasure and torment.

Her claws sprang forward and dug into his flesh. The fire inside her wanted to burn her alive. Never had anything been like this. Not even their first time together. When she didn't think she could take another second of his intensity, his mouth dropped to her shoulder and he bit into the same spot he'd marked before. Liquid heat splashed inside as he came. He swelled impossibly further until she exploded in another orgasm as he emptied inside her.

Her body writhed against his in a desperate dance of mating more powerful than she'd ever expected. She screamed, he roared and all she thought of was betrayal. *Hers.*

She realized now she'd not only forgiven him for his rejection, she'd never stopped loving him and come morning, he would remember what she'd done and the pain of loss would begin all over again.

CHAPTER
FIFTEEN

"I can't believe I missed the whole thing." Malcolm shook his head at Lucas who'd finally arrived just after Chey had run off to hide.

"Always a day late you are."

"Well... I had good reason this time." He pulled his mate, Kira, into his arms and smoothed his hand across her stomach. "Apparently being pregnant makes you have to stop and pee a lot."

"Damn! Seriously?" Kane asked, a grin from ear to ear covering his face.

"No, I'm fucking with you." Lucas rolled his eyes. "Of course I'm serious, you idiot."

Malcolm remained quiet while Kane and Lara fussed over Lucas and Kira. He was genuinely happy for his brother but the thought of Kira rounded with child made him think of what he'd missed. While he'd been off becoming the bastard from hell, Chey had endured a pregnancy without him. She'd pushed his baby into this world and he'd been doing fuck knew what. Malcolm pushed his fingers through his hair and blew out a hard breath. He couldn't change the past. Those years were gone and couldn't be redone. He either manned up and moved on or the loss would eat him alive.

Malcolm wandered into the office and found his child sleeping peacefully on the couch. Her black ringlets fell across her check, blocking her partially from his view. His heart ached at the sight of her. The past was definitely the past. This beautiful and amazing girl who'd shifted into the first ever female black cougar was their future. It was up to him to ensure no harm came to her until she was strong enough to defend herself.

"We're going to have to be careful what we do with this knowledge." Lucas' voice drifted on the barest of whispers. His brothers flanked him, joining him at watching his sweet child. "She's going to be a heartbreaker."

"She's the future of our clan. I can feel it in my gut." And not just because she was part of him. When his brothers nodded, he knew they understood. "Kira could birth another." The knowledge of that fact hung in the air.

"Do you get the sense that we've seriously underestimated the power of love and family?"

The brothers nodded.

"I don't know how we so easily forgot. From here on out, we must embrace the legacy our parents left behind. Love. Family. Peace."

Malcolm couldn't deny a word Lucas said. Chey had risked everything for Allie. She'd been willing to sacrifice herself if it meant her child would live another day. Malcolm hadn't witnessed that kind of love in his life since his parents had died. He and his brothers had lost their way. Especially him. Bran might have been the cause of it, but they'd allowed it to happen by sticking their heads in the sand and refusing to stand up to the council when the shit had hit the fan in the first place.

"No more running," Malcolm said.

"No," his brothers spoke in unison.

"We're going to need Kitty to cover our asses. She's the only one who knows the truth behind her father. How deep his bullshit went."

Lucas laughed. "Good luck with that. That bitch only knows how to help one person and that's herself."

Kane smiled. "Oh she'll help. She owes me now." They turned in question to Kane, who raised his hands in mock surrender. "Don't look at me. She pissed off my mate and she's the one with all the witchy powers. Kitty will sing like a bird or Lara will make her pay for everything she's done, one spell at a time."

"Dude. Your woman..."

Dark clouds formed briefly in Kane's eyes at Malcolm's words and he promptly shut his mouth. He knew when to stop. His past with Lara was going to be a touchy subject for a while to come.

Together, they left the office and reconvened in the living room. Kitty lay sprawled across a cot Lara had set up for her with glowing stones surrounding the makeshift bed.

"Just making sure she can't go anywhere," Lara offered.

"What's her prognosis?" Kane asked.

"Alive and cranky. Did you expect anything less?"

Two council members emerged from the kitchen, flanked by Ben. Malcolm growled and unsheathed his claws. "Who let the riff raff in?"

"Easy, Malcolm. Ben was working for me the whole time. Unfortunately Charlie was not. She was Bran's pawn and she caused all kinds of problems before Ben could put her down."

"She drugged Chey, dammit!"

Ben stepped forward. "I know and I'm sorry. Her intent had been to kill you both. She's the one who shot you outside your safe house."

Malcolm seethed with anger. Ripping out Bran's heart no longer seemed harsh enough.

"I did get a signed confession out of her before she was put down though. I've already presented my evidence to the council."

"Good, does that mean we don't have to keep her alive?" Lara asked hopefully.

"We're hoping she can fill in all the gaps from the last few years. It seems the council has a lot to make up for."

"The council should be disbanded. You've grown so far out of touch with the clan you've become obsolete."

The council member stared hard at Malcolm for several seconds before relenting and bowing his head. "I believe we can all learn from this and begin to rebuild something even better."

Malcolm snorted. He was still too close to the edge to deal with political bullshit. This was his brothers' area of expertise. "I'm going to check on Chey. She's been through hell."

Lucas touched Malcolm's shoulder. "So have you, brother. Cut yourself some slack. We've all made mistakes that we can put behind us."

He wasn't sure he could believe that. Some sins didn't deserve forgiveness. He nodded his head and left the room. His body ached for his mate's touch. No matter where he stood in this house he smelled her. A delicious blend of woman and sass that made his dick press against his pants.

He moved silently into the bedroom and removed his clothing. Nothing would come between them again, he vowed. Her slow, even breathing indicated how deeply she slept so he chose to simply wrap himself around her and soak in her heat. "You're mine now and I have no intention of letting go," he whispered into the silk fall of her hair before settling his head on the pillow and allowing his body to finally relax.

. . .

CHEY AWOKE in Malcolm's arms surrounded by his heat and an incredibly hard erection poking her in the ass. His fingers played along the curve of her hip, stroking and tickling her sensitive skin. She held her breath, too afraid to look at him. They'd returned to Kane's cabin and she'd practically run to the guest bedroom Lara offered to escape after she'd checked up on her slumbering child. Allie had always been one too quick to recover from any kind of trauma, but for the second time in her life she was grateful. After a quick shower, she'd slid under the soft down comforter and waited for Malcolm to find her. The pit of dread had grown tighter with each passing minute until finally exhaustion had taken her and she'd fallen into a fitful sleep.

Why was he still here? And stroking her skin like a lover? Surely by now he'd recovered from killing Bran. Afraid to break the moment, Chey pretended to still be asleep. Long minutes passed where Malcolm's soft touch drove her crazy. He seemed to hold her with such care, his touch light and protective.

"I know you're awake," he mumbled at her ear.

"I wasn't sure what to say yet." Goodbye was going to kill her.

"How about good morning, mate."

Chey whirled around and faced him, pulling back at the devilish grin crossing his face. "I—I don't understand. You should be furious with me."

He cupped one of her bare breasts, brushing lightly across the hardened nipple. "Oh you can bet there will be punishment coming for not telling me about Allie. But she's one of us now, she can't leave and neither can you."

His easy statement in telling her she was trapped did not go well. She didn't want to leave but that didn't mean he got to order her around with a sardonic smile and a hot touch across her skin. He tweaked her nipple again. Okay, maybe he could have his way when he did that. She squirmed against him.

"Telling me what I can and cannot do might not be the best way to start your day, cat boy." Sarcasm came so much easier than the emotions churning through her stomach. Still, she touched his face and watched his eyes change color—deepen. It was obvious he wanted her but there was so much more she didn't understand.

"I haven't changed, Malcolm. I'm always going to be—" She didn't want to ruin the moment with the word.

"I know exactly who you are. I always have. Goddess, Chey. I was a fucking idiot. I should be shot for all the years I wasted."

Tears rushed to her eyes. "Don't." She choked.

SILENCE STRETCHED between them while Malcolm tried to ignore the hunger pulsing inside him. He needed to go slow. Take it easy this time. But he was so damned desperate for her. Yes, she was still a half wolf but who was he anymore? He'd finally learned that it wasn't his place to judge. *Only took five years, you dumb ass.*

Cheyenne.

She was his. By some fluke of fate or the Goddess shining down on him for no good reason, she was definitely his and she wasn't going to get away.

"Kiss me." If she didn't he would die.

She leaned forward and pressed her lips to his in a tight, close-mouthed kiss. When he was about to protest, she thrust her tongue into his mouth and stroked over his. Fucking A.

All the events of the last several days flashed before his eyes, from the moment he'd pinned her to the floor, to her making a jump for Bran with his gun pointed at her. A wild cry escaped his throat. His beautiful blonde mate had a wild streak a mile wide that he suspected would be the death of him one day. He rolled her to her back and pressed her into the bed with his kiss.

Hard and unrelenting. With her soft and compliant underneath him, he finally had control.

He pressed his cock against her stomach. Malcolm wrenched free from their kiss and lowered his head to a hard tip of her breast and sucked it into his mouth. Her moans quickly filled the room as he stroked her nipples over and over until she writhed underneath him.

He needed her so damned bad he was burning up with it. Chey parted her thighs and Malcolm slid a finger through her sex. Hot. Ready. He added another finger to the first and thrust harder. She moaned again, this time much louder. It wasn't enough. She had to scream for him. He really liked that.

With his thumb, he circled her clit, teasing her to the brink until her nose flared and her eyes widened on the verge of coming. He withdrew his hand.

"Malcolm!"

The hunger in her voice awakened the more dominant beast inside him. He wrapped his arm around her waist and flipped her to her stomach. His gaze dropped to her beautiful ass. Round. Womanly and so fucking soft. He loved her ass. He lifted her on her knees and pressed her chest and face to the mattress. *Yes.*

"Fuck me, Malcolm. Do it."

He positioned her so that the head of his dick rested at her entrance. She tried to move but he simply held her tighter. He had control now. The sweet scent of her arousal drifted to his nose, inciting the need already blazing out of control inside him. He drove inside as deep as he could go—and she screamed in ecstasy at the same time. Music to his ears.

The hot clasp of her ripped at his threads of control, the muscles convulsing around him. He withdrew and plunged again. This time her mouth opened wide and a long loud wail filled the room. He thrust harder—out of his mind with need. The fist tight grip and liquid heat of her pussy overtook him. Every pulse of her release tore up his spine. His balls tightened painfully.

"More!" she screamed.

Their joining turned wild as he shoved into her milking pussy, slick with her cream. One last push of her ass in his direction and Malcolm erupted, his body trembled, and his release splashed inside her. A strangled roar filled his head before he collapsed forward, blanketing her with his body.

Their heavy breaths and quivering bodies eventually settled into a steady driving rhythm that comforted him in ways that nothing else could. *Mine. Love.*

The words fell from his mouth without thought. Never again would she suffer alone. Nothing could remove him from her side. Not even death.

He eased from her body and snuggled next to her, burying his face in her hair. He could tell by the lack of movement from her that she held her breath. "You don't have to do that. I meant what I said."

"How can you tell? The mating..."

"Fuck that. Somewhere deep inside I've always known I just needed to quit fighting it."

"But what about the—"

He clamped his hand over her mouth and turned her to face him. "No buts. No ifs. No what abouts. I love you. It really is that simple. Trust me, we can do this."

"I do trust you."

Tears fell from her eyes but something clicked. He saw it in her eyes the moment it happened. She stroked his face and traced his lips with her fingers. "You're not going to make this easy are you?"

He shook his head. "I can guarantee I will drive you crazy. But when we're alone..." He looked over his shoulder. "...or semi alone, I can promise you there won't be a single regret."

"Uh huh. I'm not sure I believe that, Mr. Gunn. Every time you think I've done something naughty you'll be looking to punish me."

He grinned down at her. "You're damn right. And you're going to love every minute of it." He pressed his mouth to her sweet skin and smiled. *Let the games begin...*

Thank you so much for reading!

If you enjoyed this book please take a moment to help other readers discover it by leaving a review on your favorite retailer.

Just a few words and some stars really does help!

Ready for more Southern Shifters? *Bad Kitty*, the next in the series is now available and you can read a preview at the end of this book.

If you want more information on all of the books in my Southern Shifters series, you can find the full reading order, previews and links at ElizaGayle.com

Turn the page for the first chapter of *Bad Kitty*, the next book in the Southern Shifter series!

BAD KITTY PREVIEW

Enjoy this Sneak Peek of the next book in the Southern Shifters series.

BAD KITTY

By
Eliza Gayle

Kitty stared down at the keys in her hand and shook her head. Walking away from the Clan and everything she'd ever known had been hard enough, but this...this was too much. She wasn't just some damn charity case Kane could sweep under the rug by offering an empty house in the neutral zone for her to live in. Her entire life to this point had been in the sheltered protection of her clan. Now they didn't want her, just like her father.

Anger boiled in her veins every time she thought of him. She tried to do the right thing when she found out about his attempt to kidnap Malcolm's child, but the Clan decided her efforts were too little too late. Her father's attempts to kill or undermine the Guardian brothers at every turn had failed. He'd been a damned fool all along. Yes, she'd remained quiet despite what she knew. But she didn't need to stick her neck out and bring her own father's wrath down on her head.

All she'd had to do was wait for everything to blow up. And there lay the crux of her problem today. She'd had more than a pretty good idea about much of what her father was up to and had kept the information to herself. As far as she'd been concerned, it hadn't been her place to either agree with him or stand against him.

The why of most of his schemes still escaped her, so she ignored the havoc he'd created. She'd been under the mistaken impression that, somewhere deep down, her father cared about her. But then she'd discovered the child. Her father found out about Malcolm's secret offspring and had planned to do who knows what with her. So she'd snuck the child away and out of her father's reach. Rescuing the girl had been her only saving grace with the council and meant the difference between a death sentence and *this*. At the last minute Kane had stood up for her and offered a compromise in the form of an extended vacation. Kitty chuffed, the sound far more animal than human.

Vacation my ass.

More like indefinite exile, and to the neutral zone no less. The only people who belonged here were the half-breeds no one knew what else to do with. Kitty curled her upper lip, pushed opened the door and exited the car packed with the few belongings she'd been allowed to keep. She headed toward the small cottage with the extended wrap-around porch. Maybe, just maybe, if she'd been offered a place like this on clan land, its pretty exterior would have charmed her. But here it was no more than a prison of four walls where she'd have to hide from the local residents. No one wanted a full blood feline hanging around. Trust would be impossible.

She had half a mind to take her chances with the humans instead.

The sun's rays trickled through the tree canopy that offered the hideout more privacy than she'd expected. Despite the chill in the late afternoon air, everything around her mocked her with its almost summer like beauty. She didn't want to notice the pretty poppies growing in a border around the left side of the yard, nor did she want to see raised garden beds at the edge of the property that beckoned for someone to fill them with fruits and vegetables.

They could dress it up and call this place whatever they wanted. She'd essentially been kicked out with no information about when or if she could ever return. Irritated and tired, she walked up the driveway toward her banishment. As far as she knew the place had stood empty for many years. While Deals Gap, North Carolina had officially been declared a neutral zone in the tenuous treaty between the wolf and cougar clans, they'd been encouraged to keep to their own lands as much as possible. Especially her. Her father had been beyond vigilant in his preaching about keeping the bloodlines pure and not associating with other races for anything more than absolute necessity. Supposedly everything he'd done had been in some part due to his bloodline obsession. Although, considering her recent discovery of a half-sister who was half-cougar and half-witch, she'd begun to question everything.

Kitty rubbed her head and tried to push the anger and resentment from her thoughts. Her actions of the last few years had not been great either. The embarrassment of her relentless pursuit of a man who didn't give a rat's ass about her burned through her soul like acid. Unfortunately there were a lot of other things she'd done almost as humiliating as her behavior with Kane. Things she couldn't take back or change.

She'd hole up here for a few weeks until she got her head on straight and come up with a new strategy for the next several months. Her father's assets had all been confiscated, leaving her with nothing to fall back on. Her job skills were a joke and there had been no reason to hold down a nine to five with her father taking care of everything. Kitty had wasted all her time being a stuck up bitch. There, she admitted it.

Oh, how the mighty have fallen...

Stepping onto the small porch, Kitty lifted the sunglasses from her eyes. The paint looked fresh and the area around her was neat, obviously someone took care of the place. As she slid the key into the deadbolt of the door, the scrape of metal on metal screeched through her head. She pushed the door open and the air suddenly shifted around her. The hair at her nape stood on end. Tension pulled at her skull and instantly notified her she was no longer alone. Before she could react, or even turn around, the door slammed in her face and she flew backwards. Her muscles flexed and her claws burst free as she scrambled to catch herself.

The air whooshed from her lungs as her thickened nails dug into the wooden steps of the porch, barely breaking her fall. She pushed to her feet at the same time a hard kick was delivered to her ribs and another to her face.

"Don't even think about it, bitch. You've had this coming for a long damn time and I'm going to make sure you finally get what's yours."

Black spots blurred Kitty's vision from the pain of the blows. She didn't need sight to put a face to that voice. Laurel James had been gunning for her for a very long time. Competition among the feline women for the men of their kind was fierce and often violent. This wouldn't be the first time she'd fought for what she wanted.

As Kitty perched precariously on all fours, several pairs of legs crossed her line of sight. Laurel wasn't alone. Whatever they had planned, she'd brought reinforcements and this wasn't going to go well for Kitty. It didn't take a genius to realize she'd been out maneuvered and out numbered. Now her only thought turned to survival as she struggled to find a solution before they pulled her limb from limb.

"This is your idea of a fair fight? Four against one?" Kitty spat. She needed to try and buy some time. She'd dropped her keys and she needed precious seconds to locate them.

"What the hell do you know about fair? You have dicked around with our men behind our backs, done everything in your power to hold us back in clan politics, all while you schemed with your father to bring down our Guardians. Our only protection from the mongrels across the state line. And if that wasn't enough, just when you were finally due to get what you had coming, you somehow convinced Kane to have mercy on you and were given this cozy little house to hide out in."

White-hot rage filled Kitty's veins. She fought through the pain and pulled herself upright. With one eye on Laurel and the other on her pack of stupid bitches, she slowly took a step forward. "Are you on drugs? Do you honestly think coming here was some kind of reward? I've lost my father," she pointed her finger at Laurel, who inched back a few steps. "I've lost my home. And now I'm being forced to look at your ugly face."

Laurel's face turned various shades of red and Kitty swore steam came from the woman's ears. It dawned on her that she might have pushed too hard when the four of them circled her in a show of solidarity. She frantically searched the area for her keys with no luck. They had to be here. They couldn't have just—

"Looking for these?" Laurel held up the keys Kitty had been hunting for. "Your overconfidence is astounding." She circled Kitty. "But that's okay because before we're through you're going to wish you were dead instead of exiled."

"Shut the fuck—" Kitty's head snapped back as Laurel slapped her across the cheek. Tears she refused to shed burned in her eyes. No matter what happened she would never give these women the satisfaction they sought.

"Is that the best you've got? Fighting like a girl?" This time the hit came from someone else and knocked her into the porch railing. Pain exploded in her head and immediately her ears began to ring. She tasted blood.

"I've waited a long damn time for this so you're going to listen to every word I have to say."

To hell with that. Kitty tuned out Laurel and battled to her feet, only to be slammed to her knees. Fear shot through her mind as the true state of her predicament sank in. They were going to kill her. Her last moments would involve a handful of catty women out for revenge and an ordinary house in the middle of the neutral zone. Her heart sank. How had things gotten to this point? All her life she'd followed her father's rules, even clan rules for the most part. The fact she used her father's power to cause havoc now and again seemed minor in comparison to this. The taste of bitterness irritated her tongue. Didn't she deserve better?

"For years you've used your perfect face and perfect body to get whatever it was you wanted. What would you do if that were no longer an option? Would you simply find another way to make people suffer? Or would you turn into your father?"

Kitty didn't want to listen to this. She'd only done what she had to. No more, no less. How exactly did that make her so much different than everyone else who was looking out for themselves?

"Jealousy doesn't become you, Laurel. You should know that by now."

Another blow to her ribcage toppled Kitty to her side, knocking the wind out of her again. That one came from what suspiciously felt like a fucking baseball bat. She couldn't keep taunting them if this was how they were going to respond. She'd be dead in minutes. She had to think.

"Aww, poor Kitty. You have no idea do you?"

The venom in Laurel's words unnerved Kitty. Her former childhood friend appeared to be hanging on to sanity by a thread.

Kitty tried to get up, but Laurel grabbed her wrist and pushed her down. "You think this one little tiny mark is punishment enough?" Laurel pressed painfully into the neutral zone brand on her wrist. "That being magically labeled as an outsider is enough to make up for all the torment and suffering you've caused? Yeah, you have no idea. But I'm going to show you. An eye for an eye, right?"

Laurel crouched down and entered Kitty's line of sight. Her anger twisted the woman's normally pretty face into an ugly scowl.

"I never meant to—"

Laurel twisted Kitty's wrist to the breaking point, making her scream. "Don't even bother. An apology now would mean nothing. But this..." Laurel stretched her free hand in front of Kitty's face and extended her claws. "This is what we call a proper payback."

Kitty's old friend swiped those lethal claws across the left side of Kitty's face, slicing into her flesh. The scent of blood filled the air and for one stunned second, Kitty went numb. Then the searing pain of burning from the inside out sliced through her. She tried to breathe and couldn't. Pain so intense robbed her of any semblance of coherency. Her eyes opened wide and she looked at the woman she'd once called friend as the shock of what she'd done sank in.

"That's right, little miss Kitty, it fucking burns doesn't it? Trust me, it's about to get a whole lot worse."

From behind her someone tore through her shirt and clawed at her back, arms and legs. From some dim part of her brain, Kitty registered the screams tearing through the air as she thrashed in their grip, frantic for escape. The stench of burning flesh mixed with blood filled her head as she fought wildly for freedom. Fire crawled along her entire body, getting worse the harder she fought. When Kitty's brain began to shut down, the animal inside her took over and fought for survival, clawing its way to freedom.

An idea popped into her head. Maybe there was a small chance.

"Enough," Kitty screamed. "Just kill me. Please," she begged. "Just do it. For the love of God do not make me listen to any more of your insane drivel."

The blow she'd been hoping for came in the form of a right cross to her jaw, knocking her on her ass. She prayed for a blackout that never came. The pain, however, exploded in her head so fierce she couldn't draw a breath. With her mind reeling, she almost didn't notice when the hands holding her down broke free.

A glimmer of hope threaded through the pain. She swiveled her head and met Laurel's gaze. The smug look did her in.

With the last burst of strength she could gather, Kitty charged her, moving as fast as possible before the others had a chance to stop her. Together they slammed into the side of the house with Laurel's head taking the brunt of the blow. Someone came at her from behind, punching Kitty in the side of the head so hard she saw stars. Thankfully, she managed to keep a hold on Laurel. Kitty kicked and snarled at the others as she tried to fight them off.

A fierce growl erupted from Laurel that turned into a high-pitched scream. Kitty froze for a second before she was thrown backwards. She twisted to land on her feet but failed. Her shins skidded across the rocks in the garden, tearing through her pants and digging into her skin. The burning across her face and body felt like she'd been doused in gasoline and set on fire. This was it. Her one and only chance. Kitty dug deep for every ounce of energy she could muster until her skin tingled and bones popped.

"Shit. She's changing. Hurry, grab her!"

Kitty ignored the commotion behind her and twisted to her hands and feet mid shift. Her clothes shredded and the excruciatingly painful shift finished in a blur.

By some miracle she probably didn't deserve, she was free. Already in motion, she ran for the woods behind the house. Escaping into the cover was her only chance. Cats yowled behind her, letting her know the rest of the women had shifted and were likely in pursuit.

The shift had spent more energy than she could afford but adrenalin pushed her onward. She didn't want to die like this. Once under the canopy of trees she didn't slow her pace to give them any chance to catch up. Every advantage she possessed due to her DNA was mirrored in those who chased her. She ran over rocks, roots and natural crevices until her lungs burned and she wanted to vomit. It was difficult to hear anything over the blood rushing in her ears and her heart racing. She pushed on without looking back or letting up for even a second.

When she splashed through the first river she ached to stop and drink. A new luxury she couldn't afford. The pads of her paws had split and cracked ages ago, or at least many miles behind her. When the sun finally dipped down below the horizon Kitty couldn't take another step. Nothing she'd tried had doused the fire under her skin. She slowed her pace and ducked behind a large boulder to shift and gather her strength. If they caught her, so be it. She already felt like she'd been thrown from a cliff, might as well go for the real thing. Maybe she'd get a chance to take one or two of them with her. Kitty snarled with anger so strong it ached in her bones.

Her chest heaved as she collapsed against the cool surface of hard rock. Everything ached, from head to toe. And despite the shift, which should have helped her heal, her skin still burned out of control. Through sheer desperation, she stilled her body and listened for signs of the others. Nothing but deafening silence met her ears. Even the small wildlife sensed a dangerous predator and moved on. At this point she didn't care if they found her. She'd gladly choose death if it meant the end of this agony.

Never in her life had she traveled this far by foot. Glancing around all she saw were the same trees and dirt that covered the region, but there were no obvious signs of where she'd ended up. With the moon about to rise, she'd been running so long she had to have left the neutral zone hours ago. There were only two possible locations, one of which put her in more danger than the people chasing her.

Curious about the whereabouts of the women who wanted her dead, she peered from behind her hiding spot. To her surprise, there was no one around. Either they'd given up at some point or they were lying in wait for her to shift. Speaking of... Kitty noticed her paw and front legs shaking from the effort of holding this form. With her energy this depleted she had no choice, she couldn't hold the magic another second. A wave of energy flashed over her and her cougar body disappeared to be replaced by her now bruised and battered human form.

Unlike the other shifters in her clan, her feline form was not an equal state. Without the energy to maintain the cat, she automatically shifted back to her human form. She had no idea what it meant, but instinct cautioned her to keep her anomaly a secret. Not even her father knew about this strange quirk. He'd had a long list of reasons why she failed him as his offspring, he didn't need another.

It was quickly growing dark and she desperately needed shelter, and a doctor. Unfortunately she had nothing left, energy wise, to move. The chill in the night air raised goose bumps on her arms and legs. Maybe a few hours more of this and she'd die of exposure and whatever poison they'd forced on her. Exposure sure as hell beat getting ripped to pieces by a group of she cats out for revenge. Sensitive bitches. Nothing she'd ever done to them warranted a death sentence.

Without a stitch of clothing left to cover with, she'd never make it through the night. She needed the cat to get her through this. Kitty focused inward and reached for the elusive animal and the magic that made her who she was. A slight twinge in her legs and arms made her hold her breath. Maybe...

She focused and concentrated, dug deep and willed the change. Nothing happened. Shit out of luck.

Her only hope of survival at this point would be human medical attention. She was quite certain a few of her ribs were cracked and she would be surprised if she didn't need some stitches to sew her back together again. Hell, even a hot bath might coax the cat to heal her.

However, the constant burn under her skin really worried her. What the hell had those women used on her? So much for the quiet and boring exile Kane offered her. Bitterness burned almost as much as the vile poison.

She laughed out loud, a twisted and dark sound that should have frightened her. If she had enough energy left for fear.

"Well, well. What do we have here?"

Kitty jerked at the sound of the voice behind her. The automatic instinct to move and hide left her writhing in more agony. *Fuck!* She wasn't going anywhere.

A man—no—she sniffed the air—several men moved closer, forming a tight circle around her resting place. Not human. Kitty bared her teeth and snarled.

"I thought you said you smelled a dead cat, Bobby. She don't look dead to me." He paused, looking her over from head to toe. "She does look a bit like a used up chew toy though."

"That's okay. Either way she don't belong on our land. Her trespassing gives us the right to do whatever we want with her."

Kitty shivered and forced her body to turn and face all of the newcomers who stunk to high heaven. God, didn't they know how to bathe? That slight movement forced a new eruption under her skin. Her mouth opened to tell them exactly what she thought of that idea and instead a scream erupted.

"Jesus Christ. Shut her up. What the hell kind of noise is that?"

One of the men rushed forward and clamped his hand over her mouth. In automatic survival mode now, she bit him. He reared back and she screamed again before he backhanded her, sending her flying across the clearing and into a tree. She fell to the ground with a painful, heavy thud. Black spots blurred her vision again as she tried to gather some shred of willpower to get up and fight. Again, nothing happened.

"Here kitty, kitty, kitty. You don't have to snarl at us and play hard to get. I think you're going to like us. Maybe if you play nice and do your job well, we'll let you live —for now."

Bile rose in her throat as the three men approached her. She closed her eyes against their faces as a massive surge of fear gripped her insides.

Please let me die. Please let me die. Please let me die. Anything else but this. Please.

She knew her prayers would go unanswered so she did the next best thing she could. She used the fear, pushed through the pain and agony ripping through and struggled to her feet. The men before her grew blurry. The forest spun around her. Her legs shook and she held out her arms to keep balanced. A loud noise drew her attention, but her eyesight had worsened. The black edges around her vision were growing larger and all she could make out were fuzzy images in front of her. It was impossible to hear anything over the blood now roaring in her ears.

She couldn't move, she couldn't speak and now she couldn't see. Finally her knees buckled underneath her and she gratefully succumbed to the darkness sucking her in. It was all she had left.

∾

Rafe Comyn entered the clearing a second before the battered and broken woman collapsed. He tempered his instinct to run to her assistance. The three men from his pack who surrounded her were not his favorite people and rushing them would send them on the attack. This was not going to go well.

"What the hell is going on here, Tanner?" Rafe demanded.

All three men turned his way and snarled. Their faces were already elongated from a partial shift, their arms and chests covered in fur. Saliva dripped from their mouths and for a second Rafe's stomach turned. They looked more like a rabid group of dirty animals instead of the superior wolf shifters they were supposed to be. The half beast form wasn't the most attractive to begin with. On these three, it was downright nasty.

"This is none of your business, Rafe. We found her first so back off." The gruff voice of the wolf made the human hard to understand.

"Yeah, I can see that. You've cornered a woman and beat her half to death. That's really something to be proud of."

The largest of the group broke rank and moved toward Rafe. "We haven't touched her yet. We found her like this, and she ain't no woman. She's a feline bitch."

Rafe eased forward, making sure to not make any sudden movements. He could take on Tanner and his friends if he had to, but he might as well try and be diplomatic first. The Alpha wouldn't take kindly to him starting a fight and right now pack politics were tense at best. A quick glance at the woman showed her passed out on the ground, but her chest rose and fell just enough for him to see she indeed still lived.

"Then why the hell do you look like wild animals about to attack? Are you planning to eat her?" He knew exactly what they were going to do with her.

"We're about to claim her."

Great, just what he thought. They were stupid *and* horny, his favorite combination. Not. Rafe fought the urge to roll his eyes against the cliché of these men. Not just men though. They were pack, which offered a whole host of complications he was about to step into.

"She's in no condition to be claimed. From what I can see she's barely alive." He brushed past Tanner and knelt beside the woman, ignoring the warning growls behind him. He bent down and sniffed her from head to toe. The wolf's keen sense of smell would tell him everything he needed to know. "She needs immediate medical attention."

"Nuh huh. What do we care if she's hurt? She's one of them. All the woman has to do is shift again and she'll be fine."

Rafe seriously doubted that was the case. In this condition her body should have already reverted to the cougar he scented inside her. There was something seriously wrong here. He pressed his fingers to her neck to check for a pulse and nearly jumped out of his skin. An electric jolt fired across his flesh, making the hairs on the back of his neck stand on end. *Good God.*

He peered closer for a better look. The red streaks in her long blonde hair appeared to be dried blood and the swelling on her cheek and eye were already turning colors. Not to mention the vicious cut bisecting half her face. Someone or someones had certainly given her one hell of a beating. He turned and glared at the men behind him. If not Tanner and his ugly friends, then who? She was too far into their territory to simply be lost. He ground his back teeth, knowing these idiots had found her first, giving them rights to claim her.

His wolf growled inside him, a low but distinct warning. He did not like that idea one bit.

Reluctantly he turned his back to the woman and faced the three men. It wouldn't work well to appear overly interested in her. One whiff of his interest and this situation would turn violent in a heartbeat.

"Her pulse is faint, I don't think there's going to be a claiming here tonight. She can't shift if she isn't conscious. I'm taking her to doc for medical attention, although I'm not even sure she'll live. She smells like death.

"Now wait just a minute." Tanner moved forward.

Rafe held up his hand to halt the other man and growled deep and loud, making sure to thread the noise with the full strength of his dominance. All three men looked up at him in shock. "You ready to challenge me, Tanner? I know you've been dying to do something, but I doubt this is what you had in mind."

"But we found her, so we've got rights. You can't stop us. It's the law!" The three men took a tentative step in Rafe's direction.

"I'm not kidding here. One more step and I'll take it as a personal challenge. It's been a while since I've ripped out anyone's throat, so I'm due."

They froze, each looking back at the other. Finally Tanner shrugged and stepped from in front of Rafe's path. "This ain't over. We aren't just giving up our rights to her. You can have her for now, but we'll be coming for her soon."

The menace in Tanner's voice wasn't lost on Rafe. What he'd really meant was that after he gathered a few more people to his side, he'd be ready for the challenge. This was what an alpha wolf on the rise had to deal with on a regular basis. If you couldn't prove your dominance, then you had no business becoming a leader.

"Anytime, Tanner, anytime."

Rafe turned and scooped the woman from the dirt. She barely stirred. He seriously wondered if she'd live. The cuts on her skin looked like slashes from claws and they were ugly, but turning darker way too fast. Those were no ordinary wounds.

Despite her battered condition, he sensed an inner strength that appealed to his wolf. It left him with an almost uncontrollable urge to lay her out and nestle his nose against her unmarred flesh. The underlying fragrant scent of a woman managed to get in his head through the harsher smell of whatever had been done to her. To his horror, his body hardened as her scent imprinted on his brain. It was time to get them both out of here.

He brushed past the men before any of them changed their mind. He knew the woman in his arms needed more urgent care than they realized. Fortunately, he wasn't far from his cabin and his cell phone. How she made it this far in without setting off any alarms surprised the hell out of him. Not that he doubted for a second Tanner and his crew would spread the word faster than wildfire. If Rafe was lucky, he'd make it to nightfall before the Alpha came calling.

Now Available

ALSO BY ELIZA GAYLE

Southern Shifters Series:

SHIFTER MARKED

MATE NIGHT

ALPHA KNOWS BEST

BAD KITTY

BE WERE

SHIFTIN' DIRTY

BEAR NAKED TRUTH

ALPHA BEAST

ONE CRAZY WOLF

Enigma Shifters:

DRAGON MATED

WOLF BAITED

BEARLY DATED

WOLF TEMPTED

Devils Point Wolves:

WILD

WICKED

WANTED

FERAL

FIERCE

FURY

Single titles:

VAMPIRE AWAKENING

WITCH AND WERE

Writing as E.M. Gayle
CONTEMPORARY ROMANCE

Mafia Mayhem Duet Series:

MERCILESS SINNER

SINNER TAKES ALL

WICKED BEAST

WILLING BEAUTY

BROKEN SAINT

FALLEN ANGEL

Outlaw Justice Series:

SAVAGE PROTECTOR

RECKLESS PAWN

RUTHLESS REDEMPTION

Outlaw Justice: Sins of Wrath MC:

CRUEL SAVIOR

SCORCHED KING

VICIOUS DEFENDER

Purgatory Masters Series:

TUCKER'S FALL

LEVI'S ULTIMATUM

MASON'S RULE

GABE'S OBSESSION

GABE'S RECKONING

Purgatory Club:

ROPED

WATCH ME

TEASED

BURN

BOTTOMS UP

HOLD ME CLOSE

Pleasure Playground Series:

PLAY WITH ME

POWER PLAY

Single Title:

TAMING BEAUTY

WICKED CHRISTMAS EVE

About the Author

Eliza Gayle is the New York Times and USA Today bestselling author of over 25 paranormal romance books. (She also writes contemporary romance under the name E.M. Gayle) She lives on a small island in the Pacific Northwest and spends her days writing romance, wandering the beach, kayaking or trying to remodel something. (She blames the latter on her obsession with HGTV and Pinterest.)

Before her writing career began, she served in the Marine Corps and lived a crazy life of adventure. She may not be active in the military at the moment, but in her heart she will always be that girl who would do anything to protect our freedom. She also still suffers from wanderlust and is frequently found planning her next adventure or traveling with her husband, laptop and all.

For more information
www.elizagayle.com
eliza@elizagayle.com

Gypsy Ink Books
www.gypsyinkbooks.wordpress.com

Printed in Great Britain
by Amazon